CRACKED PORCELAIN

CRACKED PORCELAIN

SARAH RUTH SCOTT

authorHOUSE®

AuthorHouse™
1663 Liberty Drive
Bloomington, IN 47403
www.authorhouse.com
Phone: 1-800-839-8640

© *2013 by Sarah Ruth Scott. All rights reserved.*

No part of this book may be reproduced, stored in a retrieval system, or transmitted by any means without the written permission of the author.

Published by AuthorHouse   03/06/2013

ISBN: 978-1-4817-8654-6 (sc)
ISBN: 978-1-4817-8655-3 (e)

Any people depicted in stock imagery provided by Thinkstock are models, and such images are being used for illustrative purposes only.
Certain stock imagery © Thinkstock.

Because of the dynamic nature of the Internet, any web addresses or links contained in this book may have changed since publication and may no longer be valid. The views expressed in this work are solely those of the author and do not necessarily reflect the views of the publisher, and the publisher hereby disclaims any responsibility for them.

ACKNOWLEDGEMENTS

I would like to thank the following people for their contribution to this book

Artwork by Stephen Sutton

Support work by Jennifer Sutton

With thanks to my Swedish friends Anja and Ulf for their help and support. Also in allowing me to stay in their wonderful home in Sweden, where some of my inspirations came for this story.

Thank you also to all my friends who have supported me during the process of writing this book.

CONTENTS

BEAUTIFUL 1

NEW BEGINNING 27

ALL ABOUT US 51

FASHION 84

FALLING 88

THE POWER OF LOVE 101

MESSAGE TO READERS 129

BEAUTIFUL

It was a hot summer's night the rain was pouring down and people were running down the street trying to shelter from the storm. Thunder was heard in the distance and the odd flash of lightening indicated that the worst of the storm was yet to come.

But despite the weather outside things were quiet at a local psychiatric hospital as the patients sat around the lounge areas or wandered the corridors unaffected by the weather condition outside. One lounge was filled with cigarette smoke as patients sat smoking and occasionally coughing or mumbling to themselves. Some would strike up conversations or fidget uncontrollably others just stared into space.

Two of the staff sat discussing previous events of the day, they then diverted to outside pursuits such as their social life. Kathy was a well a plump and big breasted lady with short blonde hair about thirty nine, while her colleague Ruth was a slim attractive lady with long dark hair and a radiant smile she was a little younger than Kathy about thirty.

Suddenly Kathy let out a roar of laughter than startled a few patients while Ruth laughed a little lower.

"Honestly Kathy you make me laugh" Ruth said holding up her mug of coffee
"Well you have to laugh honestly I have never had such a good time since we went to that bar" Kathy held up her mug "Cheers!"

Ruth adjusted her hair tying it back into a pony tail and securing it with a bobble her large brown eyes glancing up at the clock, the hands seemed to have stood still time seemed to pass slowly. Nothing was happening and they were in for a long shift, In fact the whole day was uneventful minus a few isolated incidents.

Suddenly the ringing of the office phone broke the silence, Ruth dropped her mug on the floor and it broke into pieces. Another member of staff ran to her rescue and helped her collect the fragments of the mug. She was an older member of staff who showed concern, as Ruth seemed quite nervous.

"It's ok only a mug not life or death" Ann said mopping up the coffee then noticing a slight cut on Ruth's hand.

"Are you ok" she asked concerned
"Yes of course" wiping away the blood with a tissue. "It's only a scratch"
"I have seen you in a worst state after that boyfriend of yours got hold of you, what was his name Malcolm wasn't it"
"Yes Malcolm, well he's history believe me" Ruth said standing to her feet

"Good you can do better than him" Ann said smiling "I've had a few sad bastards myself" she continued "None of them worth anything"

Ruth pondered for a moment and replied
"He was a real psycho he must have been like it with others fits of anger and inner rage surging through him striking out at everyone and everything".

"Sounds like an animal he should be locked up" Ann said frowning.
"Oh he is, ask Kathy she was with me when he was arrested".

Ruth suddenly dropped the pen that she was playing with in her hand

"Christ Ruth your nervous tonight" Kathy said with concern
"Sorry I suppose things are still on my mind" Ruth replied picking up the pen
"Have we got an admission Kathy? Ann asked

Kathy was looking shocked and found it difficult to speak at first "You could say that" said hesitantly "we do have an admission"

"So what's wrong it's not that late and it was getting boring" Ann said in anticipation of the pending news
"No it's not late Ann but you won't like this" Kathy said waving a piece of paper in her hand
"Not Jimmy the by polar or Caroline the schizophrenic" Ann guessed
"It's bad isn't it Kathy" Ruth said worried

"You really won't like this one" Kathy said she seemed very uneasy
"for Christ sake tell us Kathy"
"Do you remember Pamela Brown?" Kathy said looking at Ann
"Oh for god sake no" Ann replied "Yes I remember Pamela from ward 35".

Ruth noticed the look of dread on Ann's face and turned to Kathy "So who is she?"

Kathy hesitated for a moment and looked at Ann for support
Ann's expression changed from a look of surprise to a look of horror "One weird bitch, who brings this ward into an uproar" She paused then continued "A truly evil madam who is cursed by the devil himself"

"Kathy interrupted honestly Ann she's not that bad"
"How bad?" Ruth asked concerned for her own safety

Kathy sat Ruth down and placed her hand on hers "She has a few problems and has complex needs, she has quite a history of abuse and traumatic episodes that would turn your head honestly.

"Yes like the exorcist a mad fucker believe me" Ann said sarcastically

Kathy looked at Ann in disgust "Why don't you prepare for our admission"
"Ok but don't say I haven't warned you Ruth" Ann said walking away

Kathy took a breath and then continued to explain about Pamela to Ruth
"Pamela Brown is a twenty seven year old woman who is suffering from multiple personality syndrome or disassociate identity disorder as it's called today". She stopped looked at the time then continued.

"Her mind is divided into a number of identities which manifest themselves in many ways mainly in various voices noticeable when she is interviewed or when she is annoyed with someone most of them she believes protect her. Pamela as the host is often hidden away by these other identities and she can become very dangerous to herself and others". Kathy looked at the clock again

"You need to read her notes to know more we need to prepare for her arrival. The police have just arrested her and put her on a section 136 you know the police holding power, Dr Gilbert is on the way to the ward to meet her so expect fireworks" Kathy rose to her feet and beckoned Ruth to the office.

"I am aware of the mental health act of 1983 section 136 is when the police can take a person from a public place to a place of safety" Ruth said confidently.

Ruth followed close behind her still asking questions "Kathy what has she done this time?"
"Stabbed a man in the shoulder with a bread knife" Kathy replied "Oh and attacked a policeman, the police knew her and seeing her rocking and speaking in various voices assumed she had relapsed.

At that moment Dr Geoff Gilbert entered the ward dressed in a brown suit, a pale yellow shirt and a dark red dickey bow. He had a goatee brown beard and wore silver rimmed spectacles, which were stained in the corner of the left lens. He looked around for Kathy and seeing her began to speak in a superior manner acting as if he wanted to be anywhere rather on the ward.

"So are we expecting the bitch to arrive?" Geoff said to Kathy and Ruth
Kathy gave a look of despair and nodded "Yes we are expecting Pamela"
Geoff grunted, "I hope you are this time" Geoff was preparing an injection and then smiled "I will be prepared"
"Is this because of that war wound?" Kathy said pointing to a scar about 3cm long down the side of his cheek.

"Well the bitch won't attack me again" He said smugly
"Geoff you don't mean that, not you" Kathy said looking at him in disbelief
"I don't believe you Geoff honestly this woman has experienced so much and you can be like that makes me wonder which ones the patient". Ruth said angrily
"Ruth you don't know her so you can hardly comment wait till you do then you may change your mind" Geoff said in retaliation
Oh whatever happened to compassion Pamela has been through a lot and what do you care". Ruth continued, "Men honestly you think you can all walk over women use and abuse them"
"Do I detect martyrdom here Ruth is it getting personal because of your relationship" Geoff said looking at Ruth then Kathy

"You mean because I was treated badly by Malcolm" Replied Ruth "Are you fucking psychoanalyzing me now".

Kathy picked up on Geoff's cue for her to come forward in his defense, she peered at Ruth with a look of superiority "Ruth that's enough lets all be professional I agree Pamela has been through a lot but we need to deal with whatever comes through that door ok?"
Ruth nodded and sat herself down tears rolling down her cheeks.
Geoff put his hand on her shoulder and spoke gently "I am sorry Ruth really I am, but you have so much to learn".
Ruth cursed him under her breath "Sarcastic bastard"
Kathy gave a sympathetic smile and also patted her on the shoulder "Bless you Ruth you really care, we care too but you have to separate yourself from the patients or they will destroy you in the end".

Kathy seemed to be speaking from experience, as her voice seemed to change from a harsh to a more sympathetic tone. Her expression also changed from a sterner to a mellower look. Ruth could see this but never commented.

After a short time had passed with very little conversation and a silent atmosphere, shouting and the slamming of car doors broke the silence. The blue lights from the police van were seen through the ward windows Kathy shouted to the other staff alerting them. "She's here get yourselves ready".

Kathy opened the door and immediately noticed blood on one of the police officers face. The other officer's face looked red and angry. They were dragging a woman between them who looked pale and very angry as she struggled trying to kick them.

She had scraggily wet blond hair with a dirty face she wore a soaked blood stained dress and bare feet. She made no real eye contact with anyone but continued to shout and fight with the police like a wild cat.

"Free me you bastards, get your perverted hands off me".
She shouted
She spat in one of the officer's face and tried to head butt the other.
"Fuck off and leave me or I swear I will fucking kill you". She continued as they pulled her to the floor assisted by the nurses. She was becoming wilder until the doctor approached with a syringe trying to inject her with a sedative. She kicked him in the testicles which angered him he approached her and this time managed to inject her. Kathy then launched forward and pushed Pamela back to the ground, at that moment Ruth shouted "stop!"

No one was actually sure who she was shouting at but everyone did stop including Pamela who actually gave Ruth eye contact, she was staring at Ruth completely motionless. Pamela began to smile at her tears came trickling from her eyes. Ruth knelt in front of her and smiled back at her placing her hands on her face and catching her tears.

"Pamela your safe now" she said stroking her hair
Ruth turned her head to look at one of the officers "Remove the handcuffs and leave her alone" she instructed.

Pamela rested her head on Ruth's chest and wept

Kathy warned Ruth "Careful" she advised her and watched everyone move back
Suddenly Pamela brought her arms forward; everybody hesitated and watched with surprise as she wrapped her arms around Ruth. All were speechless and until the police headed towards the office

"Good luck with her" the injured officer said

Kathy and Geoff went to the office with them.
"Get something done about that wound" Kathy advised
"Will do" the officer agreed "And you get something done about her"

Ruth still had staff around her so Kathy felt comfortable escorting the officers to the office and gathering information from them concerning Pamela.

Geoff shook his head "why do I do this job?"
The officers looked at him and said, "Well it can't be easy, but neither is ours"
Geoff came in with a tray of water and dressings "Let's treat your wound for you".

Kathy returned to Ruth who by now was sitting on a chair next to Pamela

"She needs cleaning up and admitting there is still a lot to do"

Before Ruth could speak Pamela raised her head and looked at Ruth

"I want her to help me no one else"

Ruth looked at Kathy and spoke confidently
"I will see to her" she said
"You will need help to shower her" Kathy said concerned
"No she is fine; I will call you if I have any problems". Ruth replied "For some reason I think she likes me".
"Ok but be careful, call us if you need help". Kathy couldn't help being cautious after previous events "She does seem to respond to you, but call us ok?"

Ruth took Pamela to the shower room, she explained how the shower worked and placed a towel and soap near her. Pamela began to take off her damp clothing and place them on the floor; Ruth had picked up some fresh clothes on the way to the shower room.

As Pamela began to shower Ruth noticed scars on her wrists and torso most of which were a result of self-harming. But these scars must have been superficial compared with her inner scars, the deeper wounds that were the result of such trauma in her life. Ruth handed her the shampoo and Pamela deliberately held her hand and just smiled as if to say I know you understand me. Ruth felt as if she could even read her thoughts and returned a smile. Ruth noticed the blood and mud flowing away with the water, drifting away as if it was never there.

When Pamela was drying herself she looked in the mirror and said
"Am I beautiful now mother"
Ruth replied to her "Yes you are beautiful in every single way"
Pamela turned to her and said "Will you comb my hair?"
Pamela was now dressed and looked so much nicer and a true model, her face was soft and glowing, her hair was like

silk and she had gorgeous blue eyes. A real angel and Such a contrast from the wild cat that had entered the ward tamed by a nurse who seemed to have an influence on her.

"I have to do your admission now Pamela" Ruth said opening the door to the corridor
"Interrogation you mean" she said smiling
"We can sit and relax in a private room ok?" Ruth said reassuring her.
"Ok sounds good" Although Pamela replied she seemed to have a strange expression on her face, almost detached from the person who spoke seconds before.

Ruth suddenly felt uneasy and walked down the corridor with Pamela. She was aware that Pamela could easily turn on the other staff and attack them. But felt confident that she was safe in Pamela's presence, providing she didn't upset her. Kathy was close by in the office and others were in the vicinity too so Ruth began to relax again. Pamela noticed the other staff and hurried into the private room ahead of Ruth, she obviously knew where she was going as she had been interviewed many times, in the same type of room. Each ward was geographically the same in design making it easy for agency staff to find their way around.

Ruth sat looking out of the glass window glancing at Kathy in the office; Pamela appeared to be very uneasy especially when other patients went passed particularly male ones. Ruth still could not believe the transformation from wildcat to angel, if she hadn't seen the display from the front door with the policemen then she would no doubt feel easier in her presence now.

Kathy came to the door and gave Ruth some papers; she led her out of earshot and began explaining what had happened from the police report. Ruth kept glancing at Pamela checking that she was still calm, while listening intently to Kathy and trying not to show any reaction in case it startled Pamela.

Ruth entered the interview room and sat opposite Pamela someone had made them a drink and Pamela was already drinking hers. Ruth glanced at the panic alarm which was on the wall close to the far wall, the staff often used it in an emergency even Ruth had used it on occasions. Although Pamela appeared relaxed she remained unpredictable and was capable of acts of aggression, Ruth had also been told of Pamela's violent incident in the community that led to her arrest.

"Pamela" Ruth began
"I am not Pamela" replied in a deep voice
Ruth hesitated looking at Pamela in disbelief
"Then who are you?" Ruth said trying to understand her
"I am James"
"Ok where do you live"

Ruth had been informed of Pamela's mental health condition, she had multiple personality syndrome a condition caused by a childhood trauma which was never explored fully due to Pamela being reluctant to discuss it and further incidents causing her to go deeper into herself. The other personalities dominated her life and protected the real Pamela or host making it almost impossible to reach inside the depths of her mind to reveal the real person. James was one such personality a strong male who protected her like a big brother, Anna was a child much like her mother Sarah but stronger than Pamela was as a child a very moody young girl.

"Tell me where you come from" Ruth asked

To her astonishment Pamela put the cup on the table and brought her legs up and held her knees almost in a fetal position then seemed to rock back and forth singing nursery rhymes.
"Bar bar black sheep have you any wool" Pamela was staring in front of her

Ruth was confused by this behaviour and glanced across to the office at Kathy shrugging her shoulders. Kathy was used to Pamela's behaviour and nodded as if to say its normal for her and to persevere.

"Ok who are you?"
"I am Anna" She said in a childlike voice

"So tell me Anna what happened to you?" Ruth felt awkward talking to this child like personality; she also thought that Pamela was playing games with her. Ruth was not used to this kind of interview and certainly not used to multiple personality conditions such as Pamela had. She could however relate to being maltreated and various types of abuse.

"Do you want to hurt Pamela, or play games in secret" Pamela asked as her Anna identity
"I want to help you" Ruth said feeling uncomfortable with the voice she heard

"He plays games with her in secret" The voice continued in an eerie tone
"What does he do, what games" Ruth asked dreading the reply
"I can't tell you its secret" She replied.
"Did you like the games Anna?" Ruth asked
"No, no they are horrible games" She replied in the child's voice "He hurts me".

Ruth tried to hide her feelings of dread, as she seemed to be listening to her own childhood abuse spoken by Pamela's child identity.
Pamela looked at Ruth and could see the anguish on her face, after displaying a few more personalities the host came forward, this was the real Pamela, a most unusual display and out of character for her to reveal her true self in an interview like this.

"Have I hurt you, I really don't mean to" Pamela said concerned watching Ruth expression change at her identity Anna's remark
"I just want to help you". Ruth felt as if she had broken down the walls and finally found Pamela, but Ruth herself was feeling the strain of interviewing Pamela and her identities.

Pamela tried to speak of her experiences, but merely broke down and cried allowing her other personalities to take over again. The interview lasted an hour by which time Ruth was exhausted trying to follow a conversation with each personality as Pamela's mind rapidly switched from one to another without a blink of an eye.

Ruth left the interview and excused herself with Kathy as she ran into the bathroom and proceeded to vomit into the toilet. Kathy raced after her and noticed the state she was in, she wet a kitchen towel and handed it to her.
"Are you alright?" Kathy asked
"I suppose so" Ruth replied
"Its never easy is it" Kathy said rubbing her back.
"You never forget it" Ruth said wiping her face
"Forget?" Kathy was confused.
"Christ Kathy I have told you about my childhood". Ruth said shaking
"Oh my god I am so sorry, I forgot" Kathy realized "Your abuse, and I sent you to interview her".
"Its ok" Ruth said almost smiling "It just gets me sometimes, I relive it especially at night".
"It must be awful, you're some brave lady". Kathy said hugging her.

After this Ruth spent time with Kathy going over points that were relevant and discarding other remarks. Pamela was so complex it was impossible to know what was true and what was not, Pamela was not lying but possibly fabricating the truth, even her memory was separated into each identity making it difficult to remember anything.

Kathy understood Ruth's dilemma she had interviewed Pamela many times and never got anywhere with her. She often wondered how she ever survived in the community and even kept down a job as a model although she was so beautiful.

"At least you got further than me, I was totally bewildered by these personalities and never spoke to the real Pamela" Kathy said writing Pamela's name on the white board
"But I thought for a moment that I had broken through"
"Give me by polar any time its more straight forward mania and depression not much else" Kathy laughed and continued writing
"Trust you Kathy nothing seems to faze you" Ruth said reading Pamela's file

Ruth read about the events leading to Pamela's arrest and section, Pamela was working as a model when one of the male models approached her asking for a date according to the male model Pamela went with him but when he led her to his apartment she changed. He made the usual advances but she was reluctant to get involved and became hostile. They were in the kitchen she plunged a kitchen knife into his shoulder and ran out of the apartment. The knife was found near the kitchen door she had obviously dropped it on the way out. The police found her round the corner near a grass bank in mud she fought with the officers they arrested her and put her on a section. The statement seemed to lack detail and was one sided it would seem that she was the assailant and not the victim. The gentleman in question was treated in casualty and refused to press charges.

It is also evident that both Pamela and Ruth had been treated badly by men in the past. Pamela had been raped and her mother murdered by two men who were never caught. Her uncle abused Ruth as a child and Pamela was also abused although Ruth's uncle was imprisoned. Pamela's mother Sarah wanted Pamela to become a child model and encouraged her to perform in front of cameras, she became

a model for catalogues later her mother was diagnosed with multiple scleroses (M.S) and reacted badly to the news.
Sarah was a good looking woman and potential model herself, she was also a perfectionist her home was spotless she also had obsessive compulsive disorder (O.C.D) which made it a difficult environment for Pamela to live in everything had to be perfect including Pamela. Sarah collected porcelain and would clean every item of porcelain daily not a crack or blemish in anything. Pamela once broke one item and it was glued together Pamela was punished for the deed and made to stay in her room and reflect on her miss deed. Pamela was made to glue the item back together and never forgot it.

As Pamela had been brought up in this perfect world when she was abused she became like the cracked porcelain, her rape and murder of her mother tipped her over the edge and as a result her mind split into many personalities and now at thirty years old she is suffering from multiple personality syndrome and unable to function affectively in society without medication. She has had countless therapy and counseling nothing so far has worked effectively the only way to live a normal life again is to contact the host personality that is the real Pamela and eliminate the other personalities. This is very hard to achieve and can only be done by therapy.

Kath noticed Ruth reading Pamela's psychiatric history and immediately commented, "Well what do you think?"
"It's tragic isn't it" Ruth said tearfully
"You think?" Kathy said coldly
"So how do you deal with this?" Ruth said with concerned

Kathy looked at Ruth and noticed that she was upset, she then shrugged her shoulders and said "We do the best we can with what we have"

"We use the multi disciplinary team such as councilors or psychologists and others, but its not always successful. So you get what Pamela is and that is a revolving door" Kathy was trying to reason with Ruth presenting her with the facts.

"So the revolving doors as we know are those who keep coming back for treatment like those who relapse"

"Yes those who come in go out and return just as bad as before" Kathy waved her hand as if to dismiss them

"So we just give up then" Ruth said sharply

Kathy frowned at Ruth "Its never easy and if you think your going to make a difference forget it, they are revolving doors and always will be" she pointed out to where Pamela was sitting quietly "Pamela is one of them so don't get involved".

"She wanted me to help her". Ruth replied, "To build up a therapeutic relationship"

"Well don't expect a miracle cure or anything, she has been through a lot no doubt about that but as for a way to help her" Kathy was attempting to help Ruth understand the situation.

Ruth felt like she had been shot down in flames, she was confident that she could help Pamela, but needed reassurance that she was doing the right thing.

Kathy pointed to Pamela's file "Look we have to be seen trying to help these people, but we merely go through the motions while society crushes them and sends them back in weaker and more vulnerable".

Ruth stood to her feet and looked at Pamela who was glancing into the office still in the same chair
"But look at her she has so much going for her beautiful and wise" Ruth then glanced at Kathy
"Tell me Ruth, why did you choose mental health, why didn't you do modeling your pretty and have a nice figure?"
"I did it to make a difference, to help people". Ruth said sincerely
"Then you really are delusional" Kathy said in dismay

Ruth thought about what Kathy had said, in her own mind did she want to become as negative as Kathy. Perhaps the years of working in a mental health environment as a mental health nurse had that effect on people. But then who would help such people if so many had so much negativity. Ruth had been joking with Kathy about the days events on the ward, she was holding a mental health magazine in her hand.

"Here we are" she said confidently "Narcissistic personality disorder"
"Well!" Kathy exclaimed
"This is Geoff" she insisted
"A fucking narcissist" Kathy laughed at the thought of doctor Geoffrey as a narcissist "Ruth you kill me" she continued
"Yes a grandiose of self importance" she read from the magazine "preoccupied with unlimited success, power and brilliance" she read on
"In other words a cocky fucker" Kathy concluded
"Shows arrogant and haughty behaviours or attitudes" Ruth laughed after reading this
"As I said a cocky fucker" Kathy said laughing with her
"Believes others are envious of him" Ruth went on

"Hardly" Kathy said "he the last person I would want to be"
"Oh yes!" Ruth shouted
"What the fuck" Kathy replied
"Lacks empathy and unwilling to recognise or identify with the feelings of others" Ruth clapped her hands "that's him"
"Yes I do agree there" Kathy said sipping from her glass of larger
Ruth raised her glass "To Geoff you narcissist bastard" She then drank from it
"Fancy a Chinese?" Kathy asked Ruth
"No thanks they are too short and have small dicks" Ruth replied laughing
"I mean restaurant" Kathy said tutting
"Know I am in a totally silly mood tonight"
"I can't tell" Kathy replied sarcastically
"What about an Indian then? Ruth asked
"Smelly and sweaty" Kath replied, "Yes ok" she agreed

They left the pub and walked down the street to a nearby Indian restaurant, Ruth sensed that they were being followed and stopped for a moment. She turned and looked around but saw no one. However lurking in a shop doorway was Malcolm, wearing dark clothes and hiding in shadowed areas in order to conceal his identity.

Ruth spent days with Pamela talking to her, attending the ward rounds with other professionals hoping Pamela would speak freely and express the things she needed to, over the months Ruth proved that she was making a difference to Pamela's progress and reversed some of the negativity that had been evident over the years. Pamela's other identities continued to dominate the conversations particularly James who acted as her guardian or superman. Pamela would never freely reveal her feelings to anyone and the other identities often protected Pamela as the host.

Whenever Ruth was off duty from the ward incidences would occur often triggered by a male patient shouting at her or touching her, even smells of cheap after shave or tobacco could cause Pamela to become hostile. Her identities would take over and attack another patient incurring damage and causing her to be restrained and medicated. She even resulted in self harm driven by guilt and shame, people often said that she was suffering from delusional ideations or a persecution complex, but often these were people who had never suffered from any kind of trauma such as rape or child abuse.

Ruth did understand and somehow knew this and felt secure in her presence, in fact as time went on they became very close. Staff had mixed feelings about this, some considered it a good thing as progress was being achieved others thought it was wrong and that the relationship could be damaging. It was thought that transference had taken place causing one or the other to have strong feelings towards the other. Usually the patient experienced this for the professional, in this case the nurse. Others thought that Ruth would jeopardize Pamela's discharge by her friendship causing Pamela to want to stay with her on the ward. It is certainly evident that Pamela was better behaved when Ruth was present as if she could demonstrate behaviour modification to some degree, or have some control on herself or selves. In fact Pamela would search for Ruth on the ward and if she found her she would ask her to sit with her, but Ruth had to be careful not to show Pamela any favoritism.

On one occasion another patient attacked Ruth and Pamela raced to her defense, she hurled herself at the patient like the wild animal she had displayed on admission. Pamela clawed at her like a tiger after its prey and the patient fell to the ground screaming and covered in blood. The staff ran to both restraining both of them, Ruth shouted "Stop" and all was silent. Ruth explained the situation but Pamela's aggressive behaviour was against her as she was seen to cause the more damage. Pamela's last incident was attacking a male member of staff for entering her room, although he admitted he was in the wrong for not having a female escort and Ruth considered that he had an anterior motive. One patient really thought that she was an angel and admired her from afar calling her 'her angel', she often defended her when she is being retrained and shouting 'leave my angel alone'.

Pamela was a strong person when influenced by her other personalities or identities, but Ruth was more able to de escalate situations and normally defused any situation by just calling to Pamela. She eventually helped Pamela and earned respect from the more skeptical members of the team, some staff even called her in when problems occurred. For the first time in eight years Ruth finally felt like part of the team, confident that she had actually made a difference. Pamela is sat watching the music channel Christina Aguilera Beautiful, Pamela never moved until the video finished then waited until it was repeated.

Ruth entered the lounge to see tears rolling down her cheeks

"This is a beautiful song and video, it has so much meaning, see the underweight girl looking at herself in the mirror how sad?"
Pamela speaks without taking her eyes off the TV screen
"How did you know it was me?" Ruth asked
"I knew" Pamela replied "Look at that skinny boy lifting weights"
"I like this video, it speaks volumes about altered body image" Ruth agreed
"So many people commit suicide for this very reason" Pamela said sadly
"Gay men tend to have a greater degree of body dissatisfaction" Ruth said putting her hand on Pamela's shoulder
"Society can't accept Lesbian, gays or transsexuals because it's not classed as normal" Pamela said, "Well fuck normality"
"I agree fuck normality live and let live" Ruth said watching the video end

The ward was usually alive with activity a girl with by polar (widely known as manic depression) during her periods of mania would race up and down the ward shouting, then in her depressive period sit and stare at the walls in her room. A schizophrenic would wear headphones playing music to drown out voices when he was experiencing audible hallucinations, sometime only wearing one ear piece. Lunchtime consisted of organizing meals for each patient and hoping that no one actually wore the meal during a fit of temper, or by the fact that they had been fighting. The occasional person needed restraining as they decided to become hostile (kick off) maybe they were experiencing visual hallucinations. Patients were known to listen to voices of command as they experienced audible hallucinations being given instructions by the devil to attack someone.

Pamela had to share a ward with many different patients but seemed to cope most of the time, this was classed as a high dependents unit where people were locked up for their own safety and the safety of others in the community. The presence of psychiatric nurse was not immediately obvious because they didn't wear uniform and wore their own clothes known as muftis. However by observing the activates of patients it soon became clear who were staff and who were patients. Most patients lined up for their medication, these were administered regularly by one of the nurses on duty. Some patients were compliant taking their medication others needed prompting, the occasional patient needed intramuscular injections others ECG (Electric shock treatment) this was mainly used for clinical depression it was like a form of barbaric torture but said to be effective in most cases. Pamela's condition was harder to treat due to the many personalities or identities that some like her created in their mind, averaging fourteen or more and each needing to be eliminating in order to reach the host or the real person.

Pamela's progress was clearly noticeable as she became involved in secular activities with the wards occupational therapists; she was creative and provided evidence of this in art classes, drawing female figures in an array of costumes in connection with her modeling career. Sometimes when she was experiencing a low period or was taken over by another identity she would produce bazaar pictures, for instance drawing barbed wire fences around a child. Sometimes scary eyes that were peeping out of trees or people falling from clouds which all had symbolic meanings usually connected to her past. Ruth was one of the few people who could find meaning in her work through conversations with Pamela or her identities.

As Pamela had showed good signs of recovery, plans could be made to discharge her. Ruth made sure that she would be involved with Pamela's release, she was eager to get her back into the community living a normal life. Normality was probably not what you could say about Pamela's life in modeling as it was based on an hectic lifestyle and sometimes required a lot of self discipline parading the catwalks or working long hours on photo shoots in some exotic location. Life was not all fun and glamour. In fact with Pamela's past and mental health problems it was even harder for her to maintain a position amongst some of the top fashion models.

Ruth was instrument in helping to change all this by supporting her, she seemed to provide her with the confidence to carry on despite her history of abuse. Pamela was actually discussing returning to work and modeling some of the latest fashions. Ruth provided her with the latest fashion magazines so that she could read the latest news on fashion, some of the photographs displayed clothes that Pamela herself had modeled in the past. Ruth could only imagine this type of world although Kathy sometimes suggested that she should venture into modeling, but Ruth merely shrugged off the idea, her life was in helping others not being glamorous like Pamela. Besides Ruth had heard of the bitchy women who went into modeling and she was made to feel very unglamorous by Malcolm who constantly insulted her looks and physique. If people abuse you long enough mentally, you begin to hate yourself and have such a low opinion of who you are in conjunction with society. Your have low self esteem and your confidence goes out of the window leaving you with nothing or a sense of worthlessness.

According to Ruth the object of a hospital is to get people well enough to rejoin society; Psychiatric wards are no exception to this rule. It is just as important to help people to live as normal life as possible in a normal environment. Unlike the old institutions that locked away mad people and threw away the key, this is the 21st century where we are supposed to care about our society and the people who live in it. We are supposed to make a difference today, gone is the stigma regarding mental health or is it, perhaps things are still in the dark ages. Ruth could be considered a pioneer in the field of mental health nursing providing many people like Pamela with hope for the future, maybe she could actually be the voice from the wilderness who cries out to the people. A nurse pleading for reason and understanding of the needs of the mentally ill, offering some glimmer of hope to them while the media just produce negative press about people being attacked by the mentally insane.

Perhaps in helping people like Pamela, Ruth can show the way for others to follow in her footsteps. Ruth believed that people should think positively and make the effort to see the good in people and not dwell on negativity. If Ruth showed that she could make a difference to Pamela's life then perhaps she could this with others.

NEW BEGINNING

After a few months Pamela was due to leave the ward, her discharge was planned centered around her re entering society and continuing her treatment as an outpatient. Her therapy seemed to be a success and she had herself eliminated some of her personalities/identities and she was a happier person. It was also revealed by Pamela that Ruth actually resembled her mother Sarah and so the initial response to seeing Ruth on admission was based on this. But now the relationship with them was much stronger Kathy was particularly concerned about this advising Ruth to keep the arrangement professional. Kathy was older and more experienced, she had seen so much in her career as a mental health nurse to know when things just didn't feel right and foresaw short comings from such friendship.

The time arrived for Pamela to leave the ward, Ruth was with her discussing a follow up visit. But kr.ew the community psychiatric team (C.P.N) would be taking over, she had to find a way of arranging to see her in between their visit. When Ruth said goodbye she embraced Pamela and slipped a note into her pocket, one of the C.P.N's were present waiting to take Pamela home but was unaware exactly what had happened. Pamela smiled as she put her hand in her pocket and felt the note Ruth returned a smile and said "Good luck and take care".

Once she had gone Kathy led Ruth into the office and threw Pamela's file to one side "That's the end of that one" she said with relief.

"She seemed fine didn't she?" Ruth said sadly trying to conceal her emotions

"Yes I must admit you did well with this one" Kathy said scrubbing Pamela off the white board "Right all scrubbed off and forgotten" Kathy said coldly.

That very night Ruth went to Pamela's apartment, she knocked on the door then began pacing up and down anxiously. Pamela opened the door she was dressed in a white blouse and blue jeans, her hair was flowing down to her shoulders and her blue eyes sparkled in the light.

"Come in" she said softly as she stepped away from the door

Ruth entered and after shutting the door followed Pamela to the lounge, the room was tidy with nothing out of place. Pamela embraced Ruth kissing her on the cheek "Welcome to my home" she greeted "Please take a seat" she offered

Ruth sat on a soft cream leather settee, she felt a little uneasy as she was unsure whether or not she should be there. If ever anyone found out she was there what would they think and was she doing right by continuing their friendship. At that moment Pamela smiled at her taking Ruth's mind off her own thoughts and instead thinking of Pamela.

"I read your note and so I was expecting you" Pamela said glancing into Ruth's large hazel eyes
"I was hoping to see you soon after your discharge from the ward" Ruth replied glancing away from Pamela and looking around the room
Pamela stood to her feet soon after sitting down "Sorry would you like a drink? she asked politely
"Yes please" Ruth said looking back at her "a cup of tea would be nice"

As Pamela headed for the kitchen Ruth scanned the room with her eyes she looked at every object in the room. And was attracted to the porcelain cups and saucers on a shelf each one neatly placed in a long line, each ornament was carefully painted with red roses and gold edging. Then she noticed a photograph and walked across the room to view it properly. It was Pamela with an older woman who actually did look like Ruth it was amazing an older version of Ruth no wonder she reacted the way she did on the day of her admission. Pamela's mother Sarah was diagnosed with Multiple sclerosis when Pamela was about nine. Such a stunning woman who could have been a model and walk the catwalk years before her daughter. It was almost like looking at herself in the mirror Ruth had trouble taking her eyes off it, in fact she had been staring at it so long she didn't notice Pamela return.

"That's my mother and me taken a not long before she died" Pamela said sadly

"Sarah isn't it?" Ruth said nervously "She's beautiful like a model"
"She was my rock and guided me through my career" Pamela said proudly
"Help yourself to sugar Ruth" Pamela offered.
"Porcelain cups Pamela" Ruth said admiring the tea set
"They were my mother's" she replied

Ruth had noticed a slight crack in the one saucer and tried to cover her one finger over it, but Pamela had seen her and suddenly reacted by fidgeting.

"Oh let me change it for you" she insisted

Pamela had presented it so nicely on a laced tray cloth and on a silver tray as if to impress and now she has one item that shows imperfection cracked porcelain
Pamela began to rock back and forth as she did on the ward, she had become very anxious and upset. Ruth began to show concern and tried to re assure her, she was worried that Pamela would have a relapse and return to the ward.

"It's ok Pamela really" Ruth said softly
She thought Pamela had not heard her so spoke louder
"Pamela I am here with you speak to me" Ruth felt helpless as she spoke to her
Then to Ruth's surprise Pamela referred to her as her Mother
Repeating this over and over again "Mother!"
She then held out her trembling hands and continued sobbing, Ruth felt out of her depth but responded, "I am with you"

"I could not save you mother" she shook and continued, "They attacked you and I could not help you"
"But you were only a child" Ruth tried reasoning with her "A helpless child"
"I saw you fall against the cabinet all the porcelain fell cups, saucers plates everything, figures all smashed to the ground"
"Some remain look not all was lost" Ruth explained
"The masks remain intact all but a small crack in one" Pamela pointed to one of the masks that were painted in a pink design

Ruth looked at it on the wall it had been hung separately as if it was there for a reason, perhaps to remind Pamela that not everything is perfect and that her life was like the cracked porcelain.

Pamela had returned to that episode in her life that was so painful for her, but this time she was sharing it for the first time with someone else. Ruth sat holding Pamela as she related the full story to her from her own experience. They were at the family home when they heard a noise like the smashing of glass banging wood on wood and then two men appeared scruffily dressed and stinking of cigarettes and beer. The one man spoke in a rough voice "Get em Malcolm" he said wielding a baseball bat hitting some of the porcelain ornaments. They had made such a mess entering the premises and Pamela's mother had tried to protect her daughter by pushing herself forward in the wheelchair blocking the doorway. Pamela was thirteen and a shy, quiet type of girl living in her mother's shadow since she was abused by her uncle. Pamela got to the phone and managed to get the emergency services before Malcolm got to her, the receiver fell under the settee and was not detected for a while Malcolm was too occupied raping Pamela to see it. Meanwhile Roger was attacking Sarah.

Pamela felt him penetrate her in a rough manner his horrible breath over powering her and the contrast of cheap after shave and sweat made the ordeal even worse. Pamela explained in detail how Malcolm had raped her and she felt so dirty afterwards. She was also ashamed and guilt ridden her perfect body had been defiled and her mother's angel was no more, the porcelain doll was cracked beyond repair. But worse than this they battered her mother to death, each blow was heard and the blood spurted onto Pamela's face across the room. Malcolm headed to Pamela as she tried to pull them off her mother, but they stopped at the sound of sirens and lights flashing. Malcolm shouted to her "You're lucky, next time hey"

"Come on" shouted Roger "It's the police

Malcolm escaped but Roger was hit by a car and killed instantly, there was no trace of Malcolm and he has not been heard of since. The police and ambulance crew found Sarah dead beside her wheelchair and Pamela sat rocking on the floor reciting nursery rhymes.

Pamela was relaxed lying across Ruth reciting nursery rhymes to her a lot calmer and falling asleep, Ruth was also falling asleep exhausted by the whole event but pleased that Pamela had managed to relate the story to her maybe now she could move on in her life.

The next morning both of them were woken by the sound of the phone ringing, the sun shone through a small crack in the curtain and Pamela moved forward to answer the phone

"Hello" she said calmly
"Yes this afternoon no problem, see you then bye"
Ruth looked up still sleepy "Who was that?"
"My CPN apparently" Pamela said returning to Ruth and lying across her knees "Coming this afternoon"
Pamela smiled at Ruth "Thank you for helping me last night"
Ruth smiled back at her "Hey its ok, was the least I could do"

Pamela edged closer to Ruth's face with her face, and kissed her tenderly on the right cheek. Ruth returned a kiss pressing her lips softly onto Pamela's cheek, and felt a tingling down her spine Ruth gazed into Pamela's eyes and began to stroke her cheek with her hands whispering, "Cracked porcelain"

As Pamela kissed her tenderly on the lips Ruth's body began to tingle and her heart began to beat faster. Ruth was slightly hesitant and she finally returned a equally passionate kiss Pamela's body was also reacting to the kiss and a feeling of ecstasy over came them both. "I am the cracked porcelain" Pamela said smiling

"Yes" Ruth replied "A
Perfect ornament cracked by abuse an imperfect world"
"Do you love me?" Pamela asked
"Of course I do" Ruth replied
"I mean really love me" Pamela asked stroking Ruth's hair
"Like as a sister or a lover?" Ruth asked confused

"As a lover, as in partners or a couple." Pamela said putting her hand on her right breast and stroking her nipple through her blouse and bra

"Yes" said Ruth undoing the buttons on her blouse so that Pamela could stroke her breast properly. Pamela ran her hand into her bra and played with her nipple with her fingers Ruth sighed as her nipples began to harden. Pamela then kissed her tenderly on the lips once more and licked Ruth's lips as she penetrated her tongue just inside Ruth's mouth gliding it in gently. Pamela then drew back her face and Ruth began to open the buttons of Pamela's blouse, Ruth then moved her hand inside Pamela's bra and began stroking her breast. At this point Ruth could feel Pamela's nipples harden and knew they were both about to become lovers. Pamela stood to her feet and held out her hand in gesture, Ruth held it gently and Pamela led her to her bedroom. the room looked like a dolls house with pastel pink and purple wall paper and white wardrobes, the double bed had a pink flowered bed spread.

Pamela pulled Ruth towards her and they continued kissing on the bed, Pamela was very much the dominant personality in control of the situation. Ruth was willing to be led into submissive state in order for Pamela not to feel threatened. Pamela removed Ruth's blouse and bra then her long skirt and knickers then she took her own clothes off until both of them were lying naked on the bed. Pamela then ran her fingers down Ruth's back until she reached Ruth's buttocks, her hand were stroking her soft tender skin up and down making Ruth sigh. Ruth then did the same to Pamela causing Pamela to groan. Pamela copied Ruth's actions and the two were making love.

The couple embraced and remained entwined for hours reluctant to let go and enjoying the warmth and closeness that they shared. It was a new experience for them both and one that was special for them both, a treasured memory that would be repeated over and over again.

"No one is as tender as you, when you touch me I don't jump or back off with fear". Ruth confessed
"Have the same problem I hate men touching me, creepy bastards" Pamela said shuddering.
"I thought it was just me who felt that way" Ruth said with a sense of relief in her voice

After a few hours they both went into the shower together and washed each others body, this became a ritual a kind of cleansing process demonstrating purity and commitment.

Ruth dried herself off and Pamela sat on a chair in the bathroom gazing at the floor, she was crying
"Pamela what's wrong?" Ruth asked her putting her hands on Pamela's shoulders "Have I upset you?"
"No Ruth I am very happy" Pamela smiled warmly "We are in love"
"Yes it's what you want isn't it?" Ruth asked anticipating the reply
"Yes more than anything else" Pamela said kissing Ruth on the lips "That's the power of love"
"I feel the same" she exclaimed "But I have to go before the CPN arrives"
"O.K but come back later" Pamela insisted.

In the meantime Malcolm was contacting Kathy trying to befriend her in order to be back with Ruth. But his attempt to being nice and charming wasn't fooling Kathy and she merely dismissed him from her door. He had caused Ruth so much grief in the past and Kathy was constantly informed of his nasty ways by Ruth and the abuse she had received from him only proved how bad he was. But Malcolm was not going to give up without a fight and went out each night searching for Ruth.

Ruth spent a lot of time with Pamela at her place and rarely went home; she always avoided the CPN and never discussed anything at work. However she did seem to be distracted at times and avoided any conversations about her private life, but Kathy was her friend and she knew there was something wrong. She had not seen Ruth socially and that was certainly out of character for her, Ruth was a very sociable person who liked to go out even when she was with Malcolm. Malcolm tried to control her life and keep her in away from friends and family, but Ruth was a strong person who fought against his abusive behaviour and finally split up with him.

Ruth and Pamela spent quality time together discussing their past lives of abuse and this only increased their bond with each other. The romantic aspect of their relationship grew ever more passionate and now Ruth was fully aware that she had crossed the boundaries of the nurse and the patient relationship. There was no turning back from this situation falling in love with Pamela sent Ruth hurdling into a new direction the consequences of this would be severe.

On Ruth's first day back to work she acted as if nothing had taken place, according to her Pamela had left the ward and she had not seen her since. She hid her clothes in

Pamela's wardrobe and there was no other evidence of her being there. Pamela was equally as discreet not wanting to cause any problems for Ruth and seemed to be responding to treatment. Also Pamela had been preparing Ruth for a few photo sessions organized by her female friend Tara, she spent time showing her how to apply makeup and modeling for clothes. Posing was strange for Ruth and so Pamela had to demonstrate positions to be in for each shot, she even had a digital camera and took a few pictures of her own. They both took it in turns using the camera and posing for pictures until Ruth got the idea of modeling. At first it was awkward for Ruth but she soon began learning the moves and became a natural. Pamela also demonstrated the moves that she did on the cat walk so that Ruth could try live shows eventually. Pamela played music such as David Bowies 'Fashion' in order to provide Ruth with atmosphere, soon they were both parading across the lounge in various items of clothing as if on the cat walk.

The months passed and things were very quiet, Kathy finally approached Ruth about not contacting her out of work

"We haven't gone out for months Ruth"
"No I have been a little tired lately" Ruth replied avoiding eye contact with Kathy
"So we must arrange something sometime" Kathy continued
"Maybe yes" Ruth said hesitantly
"You might know who is still contacting me" Kathy said trying to gain eye contact with Ruth
"Not Malcolm" Ruth said turning to face Kathy and looking at her in the eye
"Yes he wants some stuff he left at your apartment but can never find you in" Kathy said puzzled

"He hasn't got anything there" Ruth replied puzzled
"Well he thinks he has and he keeps asking me where you are, so where are you?" Kathy said inquisitively
"Avoiding him if you must know, you know what he's like, do you think I liked being knocked about, abused, tormented and humiliated?" Ruth's tone was hostile and she was raising her voice
"Ruth calm down I'm your friend and I did help you when he was rough" Kathy said trying to control the situation
"I'm sorry I know you were my rock" Ruth said putting her hand on Kathy's shoulder then withdrawing it swiftly "But I hate him and don't want anything to do with that man ever again".
"How old is he Ruth?" Kathy inquired
"Thirty eight, why do you ask?" Ruth asked taking a file from the cabinet
"Just curious" Kathy said writing on the white board
"You have been with him for three years" Kathy continued

Ruth suddenly dropped the file and some of the papers scattered around the floor, she began picking them up one by one and became very nervous.

"What's wrong Ruth?" Kathy enquired in a concerned manner
"Nothing its ok, I am just tired that's all" Ruth said continuing to pick up the papers.

Ruth was starting to think about Malcolm's age and calculating that he would have been in his early twenties when Pamela and her mother were attacked,. This meant that the name Malcolm and the description could well have been him. The way Pamela described the incident Malcolm could fit the description of one of the men, the surviving rapist and murderer. But was this possible and was he capable of committing such crimes as these, he may be violent but would he rape someone or go as far as to kill someone. She could not discuss it with Kathy or Pamela for separate reasons but she hoped that it wasn't him for everyone's sake.

Ruth finished collecting the paper together and put them back in the file, Kathy finished writing on the board and walked towards the door.

"Let's have a drink" Kathy said looking at Ruth in dismay

"Yeah Ok Kathy good idea" Ruth replied sighing with relief

Ruth knew that eventually she would have to tell Kathy about Pamela and then she could discuss her concerns about Malcolm. But for now she was safe with her secrets and just wanted to carry on working and forget about everything that had happened. But Kathy seemed to know that Ruth was hiding something and observed her for the rest of the day. Kathy was discrete and thought she could find out more if she followed her when she left work, she also wanted to make sure Malcolm didn't follow her or harass her in any way.

Ruth stepped into her car and sensed that someone was behind her, she looked back a few times but saw no one. She drove down the street and hesitated wondering whether to go home or to Pamela's apartment. Going home meant that Malcolm might be there waiting for her, alternatively she could lead Malcolm to Pamela's apartment. She drove around for some time before deciding to go to her own apartment then sat outside for a while looking up at her lounge window.

Malcolm had gone to the apartment and was walking down the street hoping to find Ruth there; he crossed the road and seemed to be heading in her direction then disappeared. Suddenly there was a knock on the window on the driver's side where Ruth was sat waiting, Ruth jumped as she saw a figure peering in at her.

"Excuse me" The man commented, "Could you tell me where Wellington Street is?" He said politely

"Yes" she replied "Just ahead, the next road on the right".

"Thank you" He said and walked on

At that moment Malcolm appeared "Well Ruth you're a hard one to find I must say" He said in a deep groining voice

He was unshaven and his hair was wild, his eyes looked blood shot and his thin face was blotchy in places. he was dressed in jeans and a checked shirt.
"So aren't you going to invite me up to your apartment?" He continued

Ruth was hesitant and said nothing for a while, thinking about the men that attacked Pamela and her Mother.

"Why?" She asked her voice quivering
"Why, what?" He asked confused
"Why should I?" she said more confidently

"For old time sake, let's have a drink and discuss things" He said smiling
"I don't think so, those times have gone" Ruth said anticipating trouble
"Now Ruth you have to admit we had good times" Malcolm said trying to touch her shoulder through the open window
"Don't touch me ok" Ruth shouted

Malcolm suddenly changed his expression to the angry violent person that she once knew, he leaned forward and raised his fist to strike her, and Ruth moved away from the window and screamed. Suddenly a hand appeared and grabbed his shoulder; Malcolm swung around and tried to punch the person who had grabbed him. But the sight of the uniform and the fact that the person had over powered him by pulling his arm up his back deterred him. Two police officers stood at the side of the car the one held Malcolm and the other one was talking to someone. It was Kathy who had been near by and witnessed the entire thing, she was explaining about Malcolm contacting her and wanting to get access to the apartment.

Ruth was relieved to see and stepped out of the car to greet her, she hugged her and then looked at her for a moment

"Wait a moment" she said "Were you following me?"

Kathy was about to reply when Malcolm broke free from one of the police officers and headed for Ruth, the police moved quickly to stop him but not before he hit her in the mouth with his fist.

"Take that you bitch!" He shouted in rage
The police pulled him down and handcuffed him while he continued shouting at her "I will fucking get you I promise".

He was taken away as he continued to hurl abuse at her

Ruth wiped away the blood from her lips and stared at Malcolm as he was driven away by the police her eyes filled with tears. "I can't believe he hurt me again the bastard".

"Kathy pulled a tissue from her hand bag and offered to mop the blood from her mouth, Ruth stood trembling while she did so.

"Come Ruth let's get you cleaned up at your apartment" Kathy offered.
"No its ok" Ruth said thinking about Pamela and getting to see her
"Are you sure you're ok?" Kathy asked continuing to mop the blood away
"Yes I am now" Ruth replied getting her car keys from the ignition.
"At least let me walk you to your door" Kathy offered

Ruth knew that she would not get rid of Kathy unless she agreed to allow her to escort her to the door, and so she nodded and after locking the car they both crossed the street. Meanwhile Pamela was also worried about Ruth and was heading towards her apartment walking swiftly down the street on foot. Kathy bathed Ruth's lips and noticed her lower lip was slightly swollen.

"You need to put a cold compress on that lip" She said smiling "What are we going to do with you, getting yourself in such relationships"

Ruth smiled back as much as she was able "I know the things I do"
Kathy then walked towards the door "Well I will have to go in work tomorrow"
"O.k. thanks Kathy" Ruth said gratefully

Kathy embraced her and left the apartment heading towards her car, hiding in the shadows was Pamela who noticed them embrace. She walked up to the door and knocked firmly the sound echoed down the corridor. Kathy looked up to the apartment in astonishment as she saw Pamela through the lounge window, she realized why Ruth was acting the way she was and decided to just drive on down the street.

Meanwhile Pamela was questioning Ruth about Kathy

"Ruth what's going on are you seeing Kathy?" she said not even noticing Ruth's lip
"No" Ruth replied removing the wet tissue she had used to reduce the swelling on her lip
"For fuck sake did she hit you?" Pamela asked looking at her mouth
"No you don't understand" Ruth pleaded
"Don't I, well fuck you" Pamela said heading towards the front door
"It was him!" Ruth shouted "My ex Malcolm"
Ruth realized what she had said and covered her mouth with her blood stained tissue, watching Pamela stop and turn around slowly

"What" She said in disbelief
"He came here and caused trouble then hit me" Ruth hoped that Pamela had not heard the name.
"Malcolm?" She inquired
"Yes he hit me" Ruth said showing Pamela her lip
"Jesus Ruth I don't believe this" Pamela approached her and gazed into her eyes then looked at her lip
"The same bastard that raped my mother and me, is that him?"
Ruth interrupted her "Wait it might not be the same man"
"No shit Ruth for god sake he's your ex" Pamela began shaking and collapsed on the settee putting her head in her hands "No it's not real"
"Pamela I was living with him, he couldn't do that its merely coincidence" Ruth said hoping to calm Pamela down and convince her to stop getting upset.

Pamela sat silently while Ruth sat beside her neither spoke for a long time then Pamela put her arms around Ruth and kissed her on the left cheek. She then held her tight and began to cry, her tears trickled down Ruth's face and she too shed a tear. After a while Pamela looked at Ruth's swollen lip and touched it tenderly with her fingers.

"Anyone who hurts you, hurts me" Pamela said smiling "Its all about us now"
Ruth attempted to return a smile "It's all about us" She agreed.

The next day Ruth went to work she was sat listening to the report given by the night nurse handing over the shift. The night nurse seemed weary and anxious to get the report finished, speaking about each patient in turn describing her night shift and the behaviour of the patients. Although

Ruth was there she was not attentive to detail, but rather picked up aspects of the report and thinking about Pamela back at her apartment. She was analyzing her relationship with Pamela, was she making a mistake or was she helping Pamela to rebuild her life by helping to remove those many identities that Pamela had developed. Certainly the identities never emerged when Ruth was present, only when others were present or when Pamela was upset.

Ruth rationalized the relationship by the fact that she was making a difference and there was a marked improvement in Pamela's behaviour. It was certainly true that by ending the relationship she had the power to destroy all that she had set out to do. Therefore she was now in a dilemma and no one could make the decision for her whether to continue the relationship or end it. What was important to her was her love for Pamela, the need to be close to her and share her experiences as well as her bed. The compassionate side of relationship was only part of what she wanted; being closer than she had ever been with anyone else was another aspect of her relationship. When they kissed it was like Pamela had breathed new life into her, giving her a sense of completion and lasting ecstasy.

Kathy was not on that day so Ruth felt that she could work through the day without feeling guilty about what she was doing. She worked with the other nurses on duty; each one had continually brought her back to reality by discussing the patients and relevant activities of the day. None of the staff knew anything about Pamela or any other problems that she had, although they were curious how she got her facial injury. The day passed so slowly and Ruth was continually looking at the clock hoping that the time would come for her to leave work and see Pamela.

Meanwhile Pamela had left Ruth's apartment and returned to her home, she was equally eager to see Ruth and discuss their future together in modeling. Pamela had found photographs of her childhood as a model for catalogues and more recent photographs of modeling career. She spread the photo albums out and sat listening to music reflecting back to the shows that she had performed at with wonderful backdrops and elaborate scenery.

Ruth left work and headed straight to Pamela's apartment she was delighted to see the dining room table with a white table cloth and two meals plated up so nicely, Pamela had made a real effort to prepare a meal and decorate the table with an array of flowers in vases. Ruth looked across the room at the photo albums.

"Is that you as a child model?" Ruth asked
"Yes you can have a look after we have eaten" Pamela said pouring some wine into two glasses
"This is nice" Ruth said sitting down and tasting the wine
"Cheers lets drink to us" Pamela said holding her glass up
"To us" Ruth touched Pamela's glass with hers "All about us"

The evening went well as they looked at the Photographs and listened to music, sitting cozily together on the settee as they had done so many times before. The lights were dimmed and once they had discussed the day's events, Ruth decided to confide in Pamela by discussing her years of child abuse by her so called uncle. In reality he was merely a friend of her fathers who used to visit her when her father was out and threatened to tell her father that she threw herself at him if she said anything. So she kept quiet for years until she was older and wiser, then she exposed him for the pedophile that he was and her father attacked him one night. The man lived but never reported her father for assaulting him; he just left the area and was never seen again.

Pamela's real uncle had assaulted her and although Ruth knew her story listened intently as she related it to her. Her uncle Peter was a short, fat man who wore glasses with thick lenses and a Scottish accent. He insisted on Pamela sharing what he called their secret and visited her room as often as he could when the opportunity presented itself. He used cheap aftershave that lingered around her on her clothes and in the atmosphere
"These smells are the things that haunt you along with the nightmares or flash backs of previous events" Pamela said bitterly
"I can understand that, it's awful isn't it" she agreed.
"So called secrets that can never be revealed for fear of being guilty of leading them on"
"Dirty sleazy bastards" Ruth commented
"My life was a living hell for a while" Pamela said continuing her story
"At least my father believed me and beat the fucker up" Ruth said
"Peter lingered around for a while, then disappeared when things got a bit rough" Pamela reflected back to one aspect of the past when Peter was exposed for assaulting another child. He was at his allotment in his shed when a gang of men put petrol on it and burnt him to death. This was rough justice for all the times that he assaulted children, he

was screaming as he caught fire and had no way of escaping the inferno.

"No one knew but I saw him burn, I watched from near the gates to the allotments". Pamela thought for a moment "Whenever I dream of fire I think of him in that shed".

Once Pamela had related her story to Ruth she explained how she wanted Ruth to pursue a career in modeling with her and experience the glamour of stage work, and join the catwalk.

Ruth was a little excited by the thought of modeling in shows but was not prepared to disappoint Pamela by refusing to try it at least once. Pamela had contacted her photographer friend Tara and arranged a session in the studio. Tara was looking forward to meet Ruth and photograph her but was hoping that Pamela behaved herself and not cause her any problems. Pamela reassured her that Ruth would keep her under control and that Ruth was sensible and stable.

Ruth appeared in the studio that week with Pamela and to Tara's surprise Ruth gave a brilliant performance once she had managed to relax. The photo shoot was a success as Ruth had worn many outfits and posed in so many positions with props and scenery just like she had seen on Pamela's photographs.

"Amazing!" Tara said clicking at the shutter to the camera and instructing Ruth to move in various positions

Pamela was in the background mimicking the movements so that Ruth could see and copy her. Pamela then had a few more photographs taken of her then a few of both of them together. Tara played some music and began to transfer some of the photos on to computer making a decision on what pictures to keep and use for magazines.

"You are very beautiful" Tara said to Ruth "A natural, so photogenic and if you like I can make you a model".

"Really" Ruth said cheerfully "Do you think so?" she said hesitantly

"Yes really" Tara said confidently

Ruth took some convincing in order for her to believe she could ever do modeling professionally. Her lack of confidence stemmed from her being abused by Malcolm, and constantly humiliating her. She was made to feel like dirt and constantly insulted by him.

Pamela was convinced that Ruth was capable of modeling and both Tara and her considered that Ruth was photogenic and a beautiful woman.

Ruth had stated that she was a nurse and not a model, she felt that she had the looks, but lacked the confidence to be a model.

"Try it for my sake" Pamela said pleading with her.
"I will consider it" Ruth replied not wanting to disappoint Pamela.
"I can put you in touch with Pamela's agent" Tara said laughing
"Tara's sister Angela" Pamela said laughing with Tara

Pamela seemed to have a hold on Ruth; she was strong willed and determined to influence Ruth and keep her by her side. She hated anyone being near Ruth and seemed to protect her as much as she protected Pamela. They were becoming inseparable it was only work that kept them apart, even then Ruth was feeling the strain of being away from Pamela. She had become disillusioned by mental health nursing due to the other staffs negativity. Yes she had made a difference with people like Pamela, but the pressure had become too much and she had to think of her own sanity.

ALL ABOUT US

Since the photo session Ruth had returned to work with new thoughts in her head. The idea of modeling became ever more desirable as the routine of the psychiatric ward become more mundane. Even her best friend Kathy was pushed into the background as her relationship with Pamela became stronger and more intense.

Kathy was on duty and determined to tackle Ruth about her new found relationship and source of distraction from her work. She followed Ruth into the kitchen and made sure that they were alone before she spoke to her.

"Ok what's going on" She said in a superior manner
"What do you mean" Ruth said surprised at Kathy's bluntness
"When I left you at your apartment, you had a visitor" Kathy continued
"You were spying on me I knew it, for god sake Kathy" Ruth began getting upset

Kathy slammed her mug down on the sideboard and pointed her finger at Ruth

"I told you to be careful and you have been so distracted from work" Kathy said angrily
Ruth felt herself getting angry but remained in control
"Kathy I'm sorry if I am not performing that well, but I have a lot on my mind" Ruth said feeling herself getting upset
"By that you mean Pamela" Kathy added
"What!" Ruth said raising her voice

Ruth tried to conceal the fact that she was having a relationship with Pamela
"Pamela, what has she got to do with this?"
But Kathy knew Ruth and could see that she was hiding her true feelings for Pamela
"Ruth you have always phoned me outside work and we have been out socially as friends, suddenly you don't call me and disappear from your apartment"
"Ok so you spy on me" Ruth said in reply
"Only because I am concerned about you as a friend" Kathy said reasoning with her

A member of staff entering the Kitchen and disturbed them; she had obviously heard the shouting. "Is everything ok?" she asked

"Yes of course" Kathy said looking at the member of staff and then at Ruth
Both Kathy and Ruth had the opportunity to calm down, but the member of staff could sense the atmosphere and soon left the kitchen.

Kathy placed her hand on Ruth's shoulder "I want to help you as a friend"

"But I'm ok Kathy, never been happier" Ruth tried to convince Kathy

Ruth bowed her head almost in shame
"My god there's more isn't there? Kathy said in dismay
"I love her" Ruth admitted
"Oh shit" Kathy said in disbelief
Ruth glanced at her with tearful eyes "I can't help it" she paused "What am I going to do?"
Kathy shook her head "I don't know, I really don't know".
"The biological time machine people are said to be in an emotional time warp" Ruth said "that's how experts explain it"
"Yes but it could be transference or counter transference" Kathy said "Or the other way around you know what I mean"
"Oh the patient falling in love with the therapist or vice versa" Ruth replied
"You know how it works and you hardly know Pamela" Kathy tried to reason with Ruth
"I know about transference and all it entails, but we love each other" Ruth insisted
"Are you sure about this?" Kathy asked concerned
"I am honestly Kathy" Ruth said smiling.
"Does anyone else know?"
"Nobody not even my parents". Ruth replied
"God they will flip" Kathy said concerned
"I know it worries me" Ruth said her smile turned to a frown "I really don't know how to approach them".

The months passed by, Kathy remained quiet but watchful over Ruth; she was very concerned but was impressed how Ruth had helped Pamela. But she was so concerned about Ruth and convinced it would end in heartache. All she could do was pick up the pieces and be there for Ruth when needed. Kathy found herself in a dilemma either help her friend by keeping quiet or expose the relationship and deal with the consequences. But she had to also think of Pamela and the effects it would have on her mental health condition, by exposing Ruth it would mean risking Pamela having a relapse and returning to the ward.

Kathy felt that she should reserve her opinion and forget about the aspect of crossing the boundaries of patient and professional familiarities hoping that Ruth would eventually come to her senses and distance herself from Pamela for her own sake.

Ruth returned to Tara's studio with Pamela and to their surprise Tara had developed the photographs taken months earlier. The pictures were stunning as both of them appeared glamorous and most of the photographs seemed to come to life.
"See" Pamela said "Now you're a model"

Ruth was amazed "I don't believe it, they are amazing"
Tara smiled and looked at the photographs then the women
"You both look good"
"The next step is magazine and catalogue work" Tara said confidently
"Are you serious" Ruth said surprised
"Yes of course" Pamela said encouragingly "This is it now, stardom".

Pamela was right Ruth was at the beginning of a promising career and the months progressed so did she, from strength to strength appearing in magazines and catalogues. Two years passed and Ruth had left her job as a nurse and became a professional model with all the training behind her. But it was not all a bed of roses neither was her relationship with Pamela at times. But it was still better than her previous relationships especially Malcolm who had not been seen by anyone since being arrested years ago. Ruth never pressed charges after the last assault due to not wanting to involve Pamela in any of her problems.

Ruth was concerned about her relationship from the perspective of her family and friends and so she discussed this with Pamela. Pamela was mature enough to deal with this and agreed that Ruth should handle it in her own way. Ruth contacted her mother first and explained that she was in a new relationship and that they would visit soon. She led her mother to believe that it was an heterosexual relationship by not explaining the facts on the phone. Ruth concealed the truth until her mother was able to meet Pamela in order for her not to have time to think of the situation and stereotype her.

Driving to her mother's home, Ruth became particularly nervous, with sweating hands could hardly grip the steering wheel. What would she say to her mother, how could she explain to an old fashioned woman that she was in a lesbian relationship. She was already classed as the black sheep of the family without more shocks for the family to cope with. They thought she was odd when she went into psychiatric nursing, the whole family thought that she would psychoanalyze them. The closer she drove to the street the more she dreaded going there, any excuse would have been a good one to avoid going.

Ruth finally arrived outside the house; it was a semi-detached house with a well-kept garden. The drive looked as if it had been recently swept and her sister's car was parked close by. Ruth sat looking into the lounge window and noticed the figure of a middle-aged woman in her fifties with short cropped hair and distinctive sharp features peering out at her.

"Oh god" Ruth gulped nervously
"Is that your mum?" Pamela asked
"Yes that's her, her names Diane" Ruth said hesitantly "So let me do the talking and please don't say anything"

They walked up to the door and her mother greeted Ruth, she hugged and kissed Ruth but seemed to pull back quickly as if she had been forced to embrace her. Pamela sensed an atmosphere between them but kept quiet as requested by Ruth.

"How are you Ruth?" Diane asked in a superior tone
"I'm fine thank you" Ruth replied her voice was tense anticipating a challenging remark
"Good come in" Diane said waving both her and Pamela in.

She watched as Ruth and Pamela sat down then turned her head away looking towards the kitchen and shouting "Emma your sisters here"
A young voice called back to her "Which one" she shouted
"Ruth and a friend" she replied

Ruth's mother turned back and immediately looked at Pamela and then at Ruth

"So where is this man you wanted me to meet, I hope he isn't like the last boyfriend, what a waste of space he was" She said bitterly

She seemed to be addressing Pamela when she said this expecting a reply.
Pamela remained silent trying to avoid eye contact.

At that moment a man walked in the room and stopped in his tracks when he saw Pamela
He was a nineteen year old with a thin body, long greasy hair and a bad case of acne.

"Who's this then" He asked staring at her
"Put your eyes back in David it's your sister's friend" Diane said in disgust
David hovered round for a while then entered the kitchen to join Emma

Ruth then turned to face Pamela and introduced her "This is Pamela my girlfriend".

Ruth's mother just nodded at Pamela and she smiled back at her as if Ruth was just introducing a friend to her and not a lover.

"Mother she's my partner, we are together in a relationship" Ruth explained
Her mother stood with her mouth wide open looking at Ruth then at Pamela and back at Ruth.
"Are you joking with me" Diane finally said
"No why would I" Ruth said feeling herself getting tense.
"But I really don't understand" Diane said looking at Pamela

"Oh Christ mother what's to understand that I am gay, a lesbian" Ruth suddenly stood up
"Oh this is ridiculous Ruth honestly" Ruth's mother was beginning to shout and caused David to enter the room to see what the commotion was all about, he turned to his mother and then Ruth.
"What's all the shouting for" He asked
"Ask her!" Ruth said pointing at her mother
"Mom" He said looking at his mother who had become red in the face with anger
"Is this why I haven't seen you for a long time, because of her" Diane said sharply
"Her, she has a name, Pamela" Ruth shouted
David looked bewildered trying to make sense of the arguing
"What's wrong?" he asked
"Pamela and I are lovers and mother is having trouble excepting it" Ruth said addressing David
"David keep out of this she's obviously gone mad working in that nut house" Diane said in temper.
"Ok that does it, we are leaving" Ruth said gabbing Pamela by the hand "Come on lets go".
"Ruth wait" Diane said "Think about it rationally"
"Mum don't say any more, I've had enough!" Ruth screeched.

At that moment Emma entered the room, she resembled Diane even to the style of dress and hairstyle

"What on earth is the shouting all about?" she asked
"Your sister is a lesbian and that's her girl friend apparently" Diane shouted
"Oh god mum it's a fad she will get over it" Emma said shrugging her shoulders

Ruth walked out of the room into the hall Emma followed behind her showing concern as her older sister.

"Come back Ruth lets talk" Emma pleaded
"Christ Emma I thought you would understand" Ruth said turning back at to look at Emma
"But I do Ruth" Emma continued
"Oh yes so its one of them fads" Ruth said shaking in temper
"I only said it to please mum" Emma insisted
"Well get this we love each other and are in a meaningful relationship" Ruth shouted grabbing Pamela's arm for support
"Fine" Emma replied with a note of sarcasm in her voice
"Fine is that it, fucking great, that's your response to our relationship" Ruth was almost spitting her words out and squeezing Pamela's arm.
"Oh Ruth please you drop a bombshell like this and expect us to except things" Emma continued with her sarcastic tone "What about dad do you think he will understand?"
"No I don't but that's him" Ruth said releasing her grip on Pamela's arm and opening the door.
"He would just say my heads fucked up that's all" Ruth continued
"Oh Ruth be reasonable" Emma said sensing her mother in the background
"I am but you all have your perfect world with no allowances for something different" Ruth was struggling to open the door

"Well it is a little odd and hard for us all to accept" Emma continued almost performing for her mothers benefit.
"What a load of fucking crap Emma" Ruth replied managing to get out of the door with Pamela.

"Well lets face it you've always been odd Ruth" Emma jibed
"Well fuck you" she addressed Emma "And the rest of you" Ruth shouted from the drive

Ruth passed her father as she raced to the car in temper "And before you start you can fuck off too!"

Her father stood and looked blank at her, while Emma shouted from the door "Take no notice of that fowl mouthed bitch Dad, she's a mad lesbian".

Ruth had reached the car and opened the door, she heard her sisters remark and shouted over the roof back at her "Yes well at least I don't live off my parents, you money grabbing bitch".
With that Ruth entered the car and speeded down the road, her father remained on the drive bewildered by the argument that took place.

"You were a great support I must say" Ruth said sarcastically
"But you asked me not to say anything" Pamela replied
"Fine so I get all the flack and you just stand there and say nothing" Ruth was so angry that she stalled the engine.

Pamela remained quiet knowing that whatever she said would be wrong; she also wanted to avoid an unnecessary argument. The Journey home was long and Ruth took hours to calm down but eventually she did apologize to Pamela. Pamela also had a mark on her arm where Ruth had clung to her this developed into a bruise later that evening. Ruth cooked tea and made up for her behaviour in as many ways as she could think possible. As for her family she never spoke to them for a long time. She was concentrating on Pamela and her modeling career.

Pamela encouraged Ruth all the way in Ruth's modeling career and Ruth kept Pamela out of trouble. They successfully kept men out of their lives making it obvious they were not interested in male friends in a sexual way. Neither did they want to pursue any female relationships only each other gay males were acceptable, as they felt safe with them. As they were both beautiful both sexes were attracted to them and both often pestered them.

Fashion shoots on location were some of her favorite jobs although some places could be awful and conditions bad. Both Pamela and Ruth traveled together and were inseparable when not being photographed. They were enjoying the places, such as historical settings and tropical beaches but whoever said modeling was easy is mad. According to Pamela it consisted of long hours and hard work performing in front of cameras. Adverts were harder to get into and required self discipline and good timing to act correctly.

Pamela had demonstrated how to walk like a catwalk model giving her step-by-step guidance; she already knew how to stand like a model.

"Throw your shoulders forward and push your pelvis slightly forward" Pamela instructed
"Like this" Ruth said practicing
"Exactly" Pamela replied
"Ok so far" Ruth said confidently

"Right toes of your foot down first and most of your weight on the ball of your foot" Pamela continued "It's almost like walking on tip toes, watch me" she demonstrated the moves.
"I feel clumsy" Ruth said falling back on her heels
"Let your body move naturally and learn to smile with your eyes" Pamela instructed demonstrating each move even the required look.

Then Pamela demonstrated more footwork and then went on to legwork, visual concentration on an object ahead using a vase on a shelf at eye level, then the body movement. After a while Pamela put music on and they practiced to music, playing old and modern songs.

They practiced and practiced for months until Ruth began to do it naturally, she was now ready to walk the walk as a model. Her first chance to prove that she could perform on the catwalk; she performed in a few small shows with Pamela before trying a bigger challenge in a major fashion show. Initially Pamela was on each of her performances in order to show Ruth how to act in front of an audience. The flashing of cameras and the applauding of audiences was a little daunting at first but even this was accepted as the norm after a while.

Ruth was building her confidence in modeling and eventually performed on a big show on the catwalk dressed in the most amazing fashionable outfits. At first Ruth was very nervous, but Pamela was always there to support her and sometimes performed with her. Ruth could feel the adrenaline rushing through her body each time she entered the stage and it continued until she was back stage. Sometimes she was so nervous she was physically sick before her performance and had to learn to control herself prior to the show. They performed with top models like Sheena Moore among many others.

Sheena Moore was an established model like Pamela who started out as teen model. Sheena had ginger hair, blue eyes and a often seemed to wear green outfits. On one show she wore a maple crown, which was tied into her ponytail and a long green layered dress with various shades of green all around it flowing down in lines. One critic called her a botanical princess, which she hated and actually tore a magazine up because it was displayed inside the center pages.

Sheena was one of the models that demonstrated her hatred of Pamela and Ruth's relationship showing openly admitting that she was homophobic. One night she was about to go outside after the show and discovering that it was raining took Ruth's coat. She walked for a while and then noticed Ruth's car nearby, she had often seen Pamela and Ruth stepping inside it after shows. She decided to take out her car keys and began scratching it, writing obscene words on the door. Suddenly she heard a voice behind her and was greeted with a fist to her face, followed by a punch to the ribs after receiving a few more injuries she fell to the ground.

A loud noise came from a nearby building, which startled the attacker ran away in great haste. A crowd soon gathered around Sheena one woman knelt down and checked to see if she was breathing. Sheena was conscious but stunned and began to speak "Help me" she said with her arm extended.

The woman nodded then spoke to the crowd "Someone phone an ambulance quickly".

Pamela and Ruth were close by and rushed forward, Ruth noticed her coat that Sheena was wearing but never mentioned it. "Does anybody know her?" the woman asked.
"Yes we do" Pamela said
"We work with her, she's called Sheena" Ruth added

The ambulance arrived and Sheena was taken to hospital, Pamela and Ruth joined her and helped to provide information about Sheena. They stayed with Sheena until she was admitted onto a ward, contacting her family for her and making sure that she was comfortable. Pamela and Ruth visited her regularly in hospital after the show ended each night and took a bunch of flowers or other items. Sheena never forgot they're kindness and began thinking differently about their sexuality, she admitted vandalizing Ruth's car and became a loyal friend from this day forward.

Pamela and Ruth eventually reached notoriety when they performed in a fashion show for television called 'City on fire' the costumes ranged from stylish to futuristic and demonstrated so many different ideas from a multitude of fashion designers from all over the world. All kinds of bizarre ideas began to immerged with creations from up and coming artists with fresh ideas. Materials from everywhere were used such as bin liners, crepe bandages even baking foil.

Pamela was dressed as an angel all in white with feather like wings and pearl like sequins on her long flowing dress. She represented good and pure as she stood next to Ruth dressed as a devil woman with a red satin dress and black tights. The concept of good and evil in the show was done as part of the entertainment in preparation for the more serious fashion displays. Unfortunately because of the revealing of Pamela and Ruth's sexuality courtesy of other models, this performance raised concerns by the religious elements of the public. Fashion critics discussed the shows performance and designs some outfits were considered shabby and too casual for the show. Certain items look better on the hangers and some of the models were described as wooden or lifeless. City on fire was said to be a mixture of good and bad ideas rolled into one, although the concept of fire was good some designers were at risk of getting burnt. Clearly some of the bizarre ideas should never have left the drawing board or even the artists mind. The concept of the Angel and the devil was hardly original and demonstrates a lack imagination on the organizer's part.

Kathy was observing the patients in the lounge when she saw this performance on television. One of the patients saw Pamela and said 'there's my angel' Ann entered the room and also saw the performance.

"Oh my god, Kathy look at your mate" Ann said critically
"I know" Kathy said in despair
"She is making a fool out of herself" Ann continued
"She's just enjoying herself" Kathy replied
"Well it's her funeral and you know the outcome" Ann said pointing at the television
"Maybe" Kathy shrugged her shoulders
"I bet Malcolm is looking at this and going mad" Ann said concerned

"Well let's hope he isn't for her sake" Kathy replied equally concerned.

It began to attract the media and soon Pamela and Ruth found themselves getting a lot of attention, but not for all the right reasons. One member of the press made a point of exposing them as lesbians prior to this the word was never mentioned. Although people knew of their relationship it was not considered an issue until now. The reporter approached Ruth and started asking her personal questions but Ruth dismissed him with the wave of her hand. Ruth simply said "No comment".

The reporter was so annoyed with not receiving any information so he commented saying 'It's not enough that we get anorexics now we get lesbians on the catwalk' the same reporter was said to have hounded a model to death for being anorexic, she was devastated by his comments as were her family and friends.

Pamela read it and commented "Oh fucking hell lets go to the Land of Oz as we are apparently freaks"

"Shit what are they doing to us?" Ruth said angrily.
"That's the media for you" Pamela said clearly used to the type of news that sells papers.
"So who needs this crap" she continued.

After the show ended some of the models arranged a party to celebrate the show's success. Pamela and Ruth decided to attend and were approached by a group of male models one addressed Ruth saying "How would you like to be with a real man?"

"Why do you know any" Ruth responded spontaneously
"Oh I forgot you're a lesbian" he said laughing
"Listen you little fucker if I had my way all men would be castrated" Pamela said pointing to his groin.
"Yes give me some shears and I will start now" Sheena said laughing.

The men walked away and joined another group of women hoping to have more success with them. Sheena looked at both of the girls and smiled "That's got rid of them for a while" she said laughing.

Meanwhile back in their local area Malcolm had re emerged from wherever he was hiding and saw a billboard in his area. A photograph of Ruth and Pamela posing in glamorous outfits advertising watches stood out causing him to stand still and stare at it. His mouth began to drop and the sight of Ruth in a photograph confused him. But the biggest shock came when he got home and saw the local newspaper near his front door. The article that caught his eye was about Ruth and Pamela's lesbian relationship. Malcolm became furious and began smashing some of his things with a baseball bat that he kept by the front door. He then went out still wielding the bat searching frantically for Ruth, walking the streets hoping to find her at a local pub or club. He was determined to find her staying out all night and becoming more furious when he failed to see her. The more he searched the angrier he was getting bumping into people in the street and grunting under his breath.

Then he saw a figure that resembled Ruth and followed her, he was convinced that it was her. She walked down the street until she reached an alley, and then turned round looking behind her. She proceeded down the alley conscious of someone following her, and then saw Malcolm nearby gazing at her. She continued walking then turned again and noticed that Malcolm had disappeared, so she carried on walking at a faster pace until she reached the end of the alley.

Suddenly she felt a blow to the back of the head followed by a series of hits to the head and neck.
Before long she had fallen to the ground her body limp and covered in blood. Malcolm stood over her and stared at her body satisfied that he had killed Ruth. He then walked away still carrying the baseball bat in his large apelike hand.

Soon the police arrived and examined the body confirming that the woman was dead, the ambulance crew arrived soon after and agreed with the police that the woman was the victim of a brutal attack. One of the policemen looked at her face and commented "I know her face"

"Who is she?" another policeman asked
"I don't know but she looks familiar like a TV star or a model" He said trying to remember exactly where he saw her.

Pamela was leaving the stage when she heard about the murder, she immediately ran down the corridor to the changing room. One of the models moved out of the way as if she had a disease looking at her as if she had two heads.

"Where's Ruth? She asked
"Over there in the corner" She replied pointing to the area where Ruth was getting changed

As Pamela passed some of the models one of them spoke to another
"There's the other lesbian" she muttered
"They are causing us all problems with their sexuality" Another commented
"Exhibiting their Lesbian behaviour and ruining the show" They continued
"It's on TV and in all the papers" One said bitterly

Pamela ignored them and continued to walk towards Ruth who was now in sight. She was watching a television on the wall and failed to notice Pamela walking towards her. Pamela called across to her but she was too engrossed with the program to hear her.

It was not until she sat beside her that she noticed Pamela and then looked at her with her large hazel eyes and spoke to her in a low voice. "There has been a murder in our area" She said sadly

"A murder?" Pamela said puzzled
"A young woman our age" Ruth continued concerned
"Probably a lesbian too" One of the models commented
"Have you got a fucking problem with lesbians? Ruth shouted to her
"Yes when they ruin our show" the woman replied
"Look if it's not Lesbians its anorexics or Muslims" Pamela commented in retaliation
"Yes but you fucking take the piss flaunting your sexuality to everyone like we all need to know" said a black woman as she brushed passed them.
"What's it to you, we have rights as much as you do" Ruth shouted

"Are you being racist?" she replied almost spitting at her as she spoke

"Far from it I am talking about equality" Ruth continued

"A lesbian equal to me as a Christian" the woman snarled

"But we are equal to you, are you condemning us?" Pamela asked

"No god is, your both evil" she said turning her head away from them

"What sort of god condemns anyone for their sexuality?" Ruth asked

"I told you" she said pulling a dress off the a hanger and starting to remove her top

"How dare you quote god to me when you dress like a prostitute" Ruth said pulling at her clothes

Suddenly the woman pulled away from her and shouted loudly "Filthy slag, keep your hands off me".

But as the woman pulled away from Ruth the material tore "You've torn it now you crazy bitch".

Suddenly a fight broke out and the girls began to pull at each other and fall to the floor

Pamela raced to Ruth's aid and one of the women rushed forward to help the other model

Before long a few of them were fighting and creating so much noise a few security men came in the room and split them all up.

Both Ruth and the other model were accuse of starting the fight and were reprimanded by the organizers of the show. Both blamed each other and they were warned that if they continued causing trouble that they would be banned from appearing on the show.

Ruth agreed to ignore any comments made about her sexuality and concentrate on modeling, it was hard with all the snide remarks but she did so for the sake of her job. Pamela was less impressed but followed Ruth's lead in order not to bring any more attention to them. One of the organizers made all the models apologies to each other and told their agencies that this must not be tolerated or they would be banned. Angela rang Pamela and Ruth immediately and warned them to behave.

A month passed without incident they were still shunned by most of the models back stage and other models often used to do mean tricks across Pamela and Ruth. It was hard to ignore some of the hateful things that they said but they persevered in order to demonstrate that they would not be forced out just because of their sexuality. Gay activists protested at one of the shows giving them support as the press put more pressure on them to quit. Once again the television cameras were present and wanting to cover the story about Pamela and Ruth and their 'lesbian' relationship, it was in the news and on television programs.

Malcolm was in his apartment when he saw one of the programs featuring an interview with Pamela and Ruth. He was shocked at seeing Ruth alive and well and became very angry. He picked up his mobile phone and searched through a series of numbers. He came across Ruth's number and smiled to himself as he began pressing buttons. He then began pacing the room like a caged animal holding the phone to his right ear. Ruth was in a restaurant with Pamela when he rang her, she looked at the phone as it rang continuously.

"My god" Ruth said, "It's him"
"Who" Pamela said
"Him" Ruth repeated
"Not Malcolm not the psycho" Pamela said in surprise

Ruth answered the call curious to see what he wanted
"Hello" she said hesitantly
Before he could speak Pamela took the phone from her and stood up leaving the restaurant onto the street
"Listen! you fucking creep, stop calling Ruth" she shouted angrily

Malcolm was angry at her response and threw the phone against the wall watching it smash and fall to the floor. "Fucking bitch I'll get you believe me I will" He threatened.

That very night he went out to search for both Pamela and Ruth determined to end their relationship. He had hate in his eyes and a desire to kill both of them if he ever found them. He searched for them all over town to places where they were most likely to go. Little knowing that he was in their area Pamela and Ruth walked down the street discussing the last show.

Malcolm spotted a couple of women walking along a road near his apartment one blonde and the other brunette and so he followed them. One of them was wearing a fur coat and the other a blue coat with a black skirt. The blonde haired woman in the fur coat separated from the other woman and Malcolm followed her. She headed across the road and was walking into the nearby park and disappeared into the darkness. Malcolm walked slowly behind her trying not to startle her as he too entered the darkness, using the trees for cover. She was almost back on the road again when Malcolm attacked her just as he did with his last victim, using a baseball bat he hit her repeatedly across the head until she fell down. Helpless she was continually battered until she died.

Meanwhile close by Pamela and Ruth were heading to Pamela's apartment

"What was that!" Ruth said
"What!" Pamela said in surprise
"I thought I heard something" Ruth said anxiously
"Like what?" she said concerned
"Nothing" she dismissed the fact she heard a noise "But I do think we were being followed"
"Let's get back to my apartment quick" Pamela said leading Ruth by the arm

They headed for Pamela's apartment both of them expecting someone to jump out of the bushes and attack them. When they finally arrived they raced inside and locked the door behind them, Pamela closed the blinds and they both sat down for a while. Neither spoke for a while just sat in silence with only the lamplight used to lighten the room. They were jumping at shadows and tree branches blowing against the window. They were suddenly disturbed by the sound the phone ringing, it seemed louder than usual and made them both react by jumping simultaneously. Neither answered the phone although it was ringing for quite a while they both just stared at it as if it was a venomous spider or snake waiting to crawl across their body.

After a while things were silent, then a short while after a knock came at the door, which caused them to jump again.
Ruth whispered to Pamela "Don't answer it" she said nervously
"Who do think it is" Pamela whispered back.
"Could be anyone" Ruth said creeping to the window and opening the blinds slightly.

The door knocked again this time they heard a voice calling "Ruth are you there"

The voice was Kathy's and she sounded troubled

"It's Kathy come on open up quick"

Ruth rushed to the door followed by Pamela; they both showed concern as Ruth unlocked the door and opened it slowly.

Kathy looked shocked and gazed as she entered the apartment, she saw Pamela first then Ruth

"Oh thank god your both alive" Kathy said with relief
"What's wrong Kathy?" Ruth asked concerned
"My god you mean that you don't know" she said looking out of the window
"No tell me" Ruth said anxiously
"The Murder in the park" Kathy said peering through the blinds
"Oh my god, I knew something was wrong" Ruth said looking at Pamela who never spoke a word
"How do you know it's a murder?" Ruth asked

"Because there are police everywhere, ambulances and a blonde woman lying face down on the grass covered in blood". Kathy said distressed
"A blonde woman" Pamela said concerned
"Yes I thought it was you" Kathy said looking at Pamela

Ruth looked at Pamela then at Kathy "The second murder round here then"
"Yes" Kathy agreed
"Wait did you say second murder" Pamela said in disbelief
"Yes that's right" Ruth said in reply and agreeing with Kathy
"Pamela when you were walking into the dressing room the other day, the news was on discussing a murder that took place in an alley close to here".
"Yes and she resembled you Ruth" Kathy said trying to control her feelings.
"Resembled Ruth?" Pamela said bewildered
"Yes and now this blonde woman" Kathy said "It's too coincidental"
"You mean the murderer is after us?" Ruth said stunned
"There is one thing you should know" Kathy hesitated "According to the police all the attacks were the same man, except Sheena who survived of course".
"So Sheena was attacked by someone else?" Ruth enquired puzzled
"Yes either a man or a strong female". Kathy continued.

Pamela headed for the television across the room "Maybe its on here" she said turning on the television.
They all sat down while Pamela tried to find a news channel, eventually she found the correct program and they all watched as the camera showed the park area and the reporter announced the death of a blonde woman found

battered to death. Then they showed a photograph of the previous victim who resembled Ruth it became obvious that someone was after them and had mistaken these poor women for them. They were being targeted for some reason; the question was who by and why.

Kathy suggested that Pamela and Ruth go away for a while out of the public eye and away from danger; Pamela and Ruth agreed and planned a trip to the countryside. They went to a retreat; a cottage near a small village where they considered not many people would know them. They kept in contact with Kathy but no one else in case someone revealed where they were and told someone. They stayed in for a few nights and then ventured out in the car to a nearby public house it was situated right in the village so was not isolated. They used false names to book the holiday and Pamela wore a dark wig when she was in the public eye. They both dressed down with dull clothes and appeared poor in order to avoid drawing attention to themselves.

They kept in touch with the news through television and the newspapers who spoke of a serial killer at large in home town. The media had a field day with this and the fashion show 'city on fire' but no one suspected Malcolm for the murders except Pamela, Ruth and Kathy. They kept quiet because they thought that even if the police arrested him, he could be released with insufficient evidence. This meant that he would eventually realize that Pamela and Ruth were alive and hunt them down.

The one night at the pub the women sat quietly in a corner watching the news, and being surprised at the things they heard about themselves. Both were considered as disappearing from the public eye due to the bad publicity regarding their relationship. As for the murders the police were no further with their investigations and who knows when the killer would strike next. Ruth looked at Pamela who was staring at the television; Pamela then glanced at Ruth and smiled.

"Don't worry we are safe here" she said confidently.
"I know" Ruth replied

At that moment three women who were sat close by were discussing the fashion show, each in their fifties.

"Don't they make a big deal out of the lesbian thing" the one said
"Yeah but don't you think they flaunt their sexuality?" said another
"No wonder they disappeared" one of them said

Both Pamela and Ruth remained quiet but were annoyed at the comments made by the women. Ruth whispered to Pamela "They obviously don't understand anything that they consider beyond the norm".
"So fuck them" Pamela said "They are obviously homophobic"

Ruth stood up and headed towards the bar, one of the women nudged one of the others "She looks like one of them models"
"No can't be she's too scruffy" said another
"Yes your right besides the blonde bimbo isn't here" she said sarcastically
"True they are never apart" another said

Ruth carried on to the bar feeling upset by their comments, once at the bar she waited to be served standing by two men. One of the men looked her up and down his eyes were scanning her body stopping at various parts of her body that took his fancy. Ruth was aware of his eyes looking at her and the fact that he cut his conversation short with his friend in order to do this. The other man was also looking but was less interested than his friend.

"Hello things are looking up" said the observer
"Hello" Ruth replied politely
"Are you and your friend on your own?" He continued
"Yes we are" she said waiting to be served.
"May we join you?" he continued confidently
"I don't think so" she said waving to get the bar mans attention.
"We are harmless and only after female company" the other man said

Ruth thought about the situation Pamela and her were trying to avoid drawing attention to themselves as lesbians, perhaps being with them would distract people from looking at them and thinking of her as one of the lesbian models.

"Yes ok" she agreed.
"So take us to your friend" the one said

They all headed for the table where Pamela sat bewildered by the sight of two forty year old men dressed in shirts and jeans. The one had receding hair and a moustache the other was fatter with a freshly trimmed beard

"This is Alan" said the one "and I am Jim" he continued

"This is Pamela and I am Ruth" she said smiling and feeling a little uneasy in their presence.
"So are you two local?" Pamela asked trying to make conversation
"Yes we are from the next village" Jim said
We are farm hands" Alan said looking at Pamela as he did at Ruth at the bar

Pamela felt more uneasy than Ruth as she avoided eye contact with Alan,

"So where are you two from?" Alan asked inquisitively
Ruth looked at Pamela and replied "South London" she said trying to avoid saying exactly where they were from
"That's a bit vague" Jim said looking at Alan "Don't you think mate?"
"yeah so what do you do in South London" Jim asked hoping to gain more information from them.
"She's a photographer" Ruth said pointing at Pamela "And I am nurse"
"A nurse, useful to have you around" Alan said smirking
"Yes if your mentally ill" Ruth said laughing "I am a psychiatric nurse"

Alan and Pamela laughed with Ruth but Jim seemed less amused as if she had insulted him. Ruth detected a look of disappointment in Jims expression and his behaviour appeared a little strange afterwards. Pamela was oblivious of all the activity and leaned towards Ruth "I need the toilet" she said tapping her foot under the table. Ruth realized what she was doing and replied "Yes I will join you"

Once in the toilet Pamela gazed in the mirror "I prefer to be blonde" she announced

"Yes you look better as a blonde" Ruth agreed

"Those men are creeps" Pamela said

"I know especially Alan did you see how he looked at us" Ruth said

"So why invite them to our table" Pamela said confused

"Because of them women near us, they thought they recognized me on television" Ruth explained

"So what if they did, I don't understand" Pamela continued

"Well they are expecting a couple of lesbian's one blonde and one dark haired"

"I am wearing a wig" Pamela pointed to her hair

"Yes but if we have men with us that will throw them off the scent" Ruth explained

"I see your point but you could have gone for less creepy ones" Pamela said laughing

"That Alan is creepy but Jim seems ok" Ruth said also laughing

"Well I think we should move on and ditch them" Pamela said with a more serious tone

"That Jim seems to be worried about me being a psychiatric nurse like he has something to hide" Ruth said concerned.

"He is probably an escaped patient, a schizophrenic or by polar maybe" Pamela said laughing

"Just our luck, to get mixed up with a schizophrenic". Ruth said laughing with her.

"So what do we do?" Pamela asked

"Get rid of them somehow, we don't need complications now" Ruth said

They both left the toilets and returned to the Alan and Jim at the table, Ruth was worried that one have them may have slipped something in her drink and deliberately knocked it over Pamela looked at what she had done and didn't touch hers. Jim looked at Alan then at the women with a disappointed look in his eyes.

"Let me buy you another" Jim offered
"No thanks" Ruth replied
"But I insist" Jim said sternly
"Well I insist you don't" Ruth replied abruptly

At that moment one of the women sat opposite shouted across to them "Jimmy Clark behave yourself with those women or I will have to tell your wife"

"Fuck you Janet we are only having fun" Jim replied

Janet stood up and approached the table followed by the other women who also seemed to know the men.

"I think you women need to know these men are scoundrels" Janet said loudly
"Why don't you tell the whole pub Janet you slag" Alan said nastily
"Well at least I'm not a pervert like you" Janet said abruptly
"We should go" Ruth said picking up her coat
"Don't go ladies" Jim said disappointed
"We have to go we are traveling on tomorrow" Pamela said lifting her coat from her seat

One of the women watched as Alan grabbed her by the arm; Pamela took her drink and poured it over his head.

Janet began to laugh which annoyed Alan and he got up quickly as if he was going to hit her instead he grabbed her by the hair and her wig came off. Alan stood shocked and all went silent in the pub. All the women looked at each other and Jim looked directly into Pamela's eyes.

"It's them" Jim said in shock
"Who" Alan shouted
"The lesbians" Janet said laughing "You daft fuckers you have been chatting up lesbians"

Pamela and Ruth made a swift exit feeling the eyes of ridicule on their backs, while the men stood embarrassed by their experience. The women kept the men occupied while Pamela and Ruth drove off relieved that they would never see any of them again.

The next morning they moved on traveling further up country to a more excluded spot and spent the remainder of their holiday in quiet seclusion. They stayed at a guest house a few miles from the nearest village. They enjoyed their experiences of nature and even skinny dipping in a lake. Pamela was the first to strip off her clothes and jump into the water, Ruth was reluctant but eventually removed her clothes and joined Pamela in the lake. Only the birds and other wild life could disturb their peace, as they savored the moments of ecstasy in each other's company. Watching the autumn trees expel their leaves and fall around the couple that were lying on the ground still naked.

"I wish moments like these could last forever" Pamela said holding Ruth's hand
"I wish time would stop still" Pamela replied

"I love the quietness and the gentle breeze swaying the trees and blowing the leaves across the fields" Ruth said with a sigh
"You're such a romantic" Pamela said leaning over to kiss Ruth on the lips.
Ruth moved her head forward and met Pamela's lips with her own; they shared a passionate kiss then lay holding each other closely. Neither of them wanted to move but eventually they had to get dressed and return to their guest house.

There were a few places of interest such as castles and museums. In the towns Pamela and Ruth visited the local pubs and restaurants without being recognized. The small cafes and shops were very inviting with friendly people and interesting items such as pottery, souvenirs and of course porcelain. They felt free as they walked down the streets but always expected someone to recognize them and ruin their holiday together. However nothing did happen and they enjoyed what time they had left without interruption.

FASHION

It was soon time to return to reality facing the world once more and all the prejudice remarks concerning Pamela and Ruth's sexuality. Since their absence a young female model that Pamela knew had committed suicide, she was anorexic and couldn't take any more publicity concerning her condition. Her life had been followed by one reporter after another each wanting their pound of flesh, hounding her for more information about her condition.

This type of thing was not uncommon in the modeling profession, Models were under pressure to look good and stay slim no matter what the cost. And the media would find a story' no matter who they hurt in the process and to hell with the consequences, many victims fell by the wayside as one more statistic. People became objects of ridicule because of daring to be different in the eyes of the general public, even today in the so-called modern world. Anything goes in fashion unless it offends the media or perhaps politicians.

It is also widely known that in the world of fashion models tend to compete for popularity and it becomes a dog eat dog profession. Often in the background of the glitter and glamour of showbiz comes bitchiness and jealousy everybody wants to be in the limelight and outshine the rest. Of course as in any profession a minority of genuine people become trampled on in their effort to establish a career for themselves, as short lived as it is. Although most of the models appeared to be competitive, some of them were enjoying being in front of the audience and cameras, and less interested in being the best. The other problem was the drug addiction and wild parties this caused many models to fall by the way side, it was all about coping with pressure some could and others suffered.

Models had assembled to practice some moves on the catwalk prior to the fashion show,. David Bowie's song 'Fashion' could be heard in the background as well as other classic songs such as Michael Jackson's 'Billy Jean' also Kraftwerk's 'Model'. Many of the organizers were discussing the props and equipment to be used for the show. A few models began to parade up and down, but soon stopped because of the lack of attention that they were receiving. One of the male organizers was extremely camp and began to display his displeasure of one particular model, by dismissing her out of his way. He was also not happy about the lighting suggesting that it was too bright and needing to be dimmed.

The press wanted to get stories about the fashion show, as early as possible in order to bring any relevant news to the public about any latest scandal. The organizers equally wanted publicity but to promote the show and sell the designs to the right people. Some people were very good at stealing ideas from others, so people tried to keep things under wraps. The fashion guru's became nervous just before a show was going to be organized for this reason. Some of the finest artist's were in the fashion industry working hard to perfect the best drawings for the clothes manufacturers to produce properly. The cloth had to be as close to the idea as possible and appeal to the imagination of the public by use of colour, texture and correct material.

Pamela and Ruth were back in the middle of the fashion world, but hiding away from the press for fear of being noticed by unsavory characters like Malcolm who was seeking to harm them. They got hate mail from people who were clearly homophobic, judging by the content of the letters. Threatening to harm them or worse, the details could be quite graphic and sinister.

Ruth discussed mental health nursing with some of the models, demonstrating the type of illnesses she used to nurse. She would never discuss patient's names of course just a few examples of the situations that she encountered, she thought it might help them to understand mental health more easily

"One woman was by polar you know manic depression, they are either high as a kite or down in a deep depression". Ruth took a breath "Well one woman while in her manic state wanted to be a model, she went out and bought loads of clothes with her credit card". Ruth explained. "She got size ten clothes but she was size 20 plus"
"No way" Sheena commented, "She was fat, and wanted to be a model"
"Yes but she was delusional" Ruth said sadly.
"How bad is that" another model commented "Sorry I mean how sad is that".

Pamela always disappeared when Ruth discussed mental health not wanting to listen to anything that would remind her of her days spent in hospital. The patient that called her the angel, who claimed she saw a halo over her head, freaked her out. Ruth also remembered the time when Sheena was attacked Pamela went missing and appeared with Ruth when they were by Ruth's car. Perhaps Pamela had experienced one of identities protecting Ruth's car from being damage. James her male identity could have taken control and done this. Ruth was quite concerned about this as Pamela could have moments where an identity would emerge occasionally.

Pamela continued to guide Ruth through the steps of walking the walk on the stage and platforms, showing her how to walk gracefully as Pamela's mother and friends taught her. She demonstrated facial expressions and turning in style. Gloria, a friend of Pamela's who also grew up in modeling, also guided Ruth. A beautiful Asian girl called Leeja demonstrated self-control. She walked the catwalk with discipline as she modeled some very interesting eastern styles. A few Russian girls demonstrated a few ideas from their designers from places like Moscow and other Russian cities.

They were working away from home so that was one blessing; Kathy had contacted Ruth to re assure her that all was well. Malcolm had obviously gone underground lurking beneath the soil with his slimy friends the worms, in other words he was with his friends in the gutter. However although he was hiding away, he was mapping out how he was going to kill them both.

FALLING

Ruth was becoming despondent with the fashion world while Pamela was oblivious to her need to get away from the limelight and continued to perform for the cameras. Pamela had spent most of her life as a model so everything came natural to her; even the bitchy remarks never fazed her.

Ruth could feel herself sinking into some deep boggy mire and was drifting from Pamela's clutches fast. Even the fact that many people continually referred to them as a couple, she didn't feel as close as she did when they were on holiday. Pamela was encouraged to do many solo performances, which boosted her ego, she was chosen because of her blonde hair and outstanding beauty. The sound of David Bowies 'Fashion' boomed out of powerful speakers and the parade continued, with Pamela leading the parade of models onto the catwalk.

Ruth had time to reflect on the past, which wasn't a good thing; she was dwelling on her life with Malcolm and thinking negative thoughts. Pamela had become the stronger person with her sights set on more positive things such as the next job and holidays abroad. As Ruth started to lose her sense of direction she began to shrink into a depressive state, her mind spiraled down in to a dark pit or tunnel. She began to feel lost, alone and sinking as if she were being pulled into a swamp.

Ruth thought back to when she was receiving counseling; she was sat in a room with a middle aged woman who questionably was going by text book terminology and had never experienced being abused in any way. She was a very smart and clean lady who probably had no vices or appeared to be someone from a good family.
She was obviously trained to do her job and that's all it was to her, a job.

She went through a few counselors and each one came out with the immortal words 'How does it make you feel' In which she was dying to say 'How the fuck do you think it make me feel'. Instead she would cry and the councilor would offer her a tissue, that was the extent of her sympathy, Ruth later discovered from her nurse training about keeping a professional distance. Ruth also hated those moments of silence that seemed to last hours although it was a few minutes, how she wanted to scream or swear at this time.

Eventually Ruth was sent to a psychotherapist who she did manage to connect with, She then discussed her nightmares and the aspects of abuse that she felt comfortable telling. It was very painful but she discussed the various physical and mental abuse, the fear of not wanting to go to sleep because of the night terrors. She hated people who hid their face behind masks or wore strong makeup this indicated the need to hide their identity. Then came the flashbacks or reminders of past events, faces reminded her certain people she hated, smells or types of clothing worn by some men played on her mind.

Ruth only had Kathy at one time to talk to about aspects of her past, but even she didn't know the full story, much of Ruth's life was locked inside her head. Pamela knew a little but Ruth always kept things from her for fear of causing Pamela to relapse. So she learned to cope with the burden of knowing just how bad it was, the only time things really returned was when she was feeling low like the present time. Malcolm could never help her when she used to wake up screaming or punching the wall, or self-harming in her sleep finding unexplained scratches on her body, when she would claw at herself. Malcolm just grunted and left the bed; he was discovered in the morning on the settee.

Kathy knew about the abuse from her childhood and from Malcolm who used to abuse her mentally and physically. She would often go to work with marks on her from Malcolm and she would make up some excuse until she finally had enough and threw him out of her apartment. He was also very possessive and jealous going into mood swings if she even spoke to somebody else, often the fights between Malcolm and her were about her going out with Kathy.

Ruth was finding it difficult functioning, she was not able to get up in the mornings to attend the shows and wanted some sort of relief from the stress that she was under. She would do anything to stop the pain from stomach cramps or mental torment. Pamela was on a high with her modeling so Ruth was reluctant to tell her at this point. Although the signs were there Pamela didn't see them.

By the time Pamela realized what was happening to Ruth it was too late, Ruth had cut her wrists and was bleeding badly. Pamela entered the hotel room just in time; she soaked towels and wrapped them around her wrist. She then phoned the emergency services for assistance, hoping that they would arrive in time. They arrived soon after rendering assistance to Ruth and gathering details from Pamela. Ruth entered the ambulance escorted by Pamela who by now was getting very anxious.

Ruth was taken straight into a booth in casualty a sight that Pamela was used to. Rachel had only seen it as a mental health student years ago with the psychiatric liaison team. Pamela sat beside Ruth holding her right hand and talking to her. Casualty was busy that night with staff rushing around and patients filling the cubicles or waiting room.

Pamela thought back to her many admissions the atmosphere was the same, doctors and nurses standing around a desk-discussing patients. Ambulance drivers coming in with newly admitted patients on stretchers or in wheelchairs. The Staff were gathering information from people such as patients, patient relatives and friends.
The whole atmosphere was completely clinical and so impersonal or so it seemed.

"Look at them Pamela rushing about, we are the last ones they want to help" Ruth said bitterly
"What do you mean?" Pamela asked
"The fucking self harmers that's what I mean" Ruth said sharply "They think that I have attempted suicide just because I've cut my fucking wrists"
"Calm down Ruth please" Pamela pleaded

"Don't they realise people self harm to relieve themselves of stress or tension" Ruth continued "Its to reduce physiological and psychological tension rapidly"

"This is casualty they never do understand mental health issues" Pamela said

"Fuck it hurts" Ruth said holding her wrists

"They will be here shortly" Pamela said reassuringly

"Yes they will and cleanse my wounds without anaesthetics and wont care how they dress my arm because I'm a self harmer or mental health patient."

"Come on Ruth this is fucking stupid keep calm or I am off" Pamela shouted

At that moment a nurse opened the curtains and called into them "Could you please keep the noise down, there are sick people in here you know"

"Sorry" Ruth said looking at Pamela "I am really"

"I know you are" Pamela said smiling

"Why can't just me and you exist in this world, why all the work and complications" Ruth said sobbing

Pamela put her arm around her "Life has to go on and I have had set backs too"

"Yes you have sometimes I forget when your up there on the catwalk confidently walking along" Ruth replied

"I have set backs or as you would say relapses, lose my memory and do all kinds of bizarre things" Pamela said reassuring Ruth.

"I suppose we help each other in many ways" Ruth said in a merrier tone

"fighting the demons and monster's From our nightmares" Pamela said kissing Ruth on the forehead.

"Make love our goal" Ruth replied confidently.

Once the doctor had seen Ruth and her wounds cleaned and dressed by the nurse she waited for the psychiatric liaison team for their part of her treatment. It seemed like hours before they came and they didn't disappoint her with their usual questions of why she did it and was it intentional. They then asked more probing questions, such as information about her psychiatric history or personal life.

She spoke to Pamela first apologizing for her actions and letting her down. Pamela understood although she was shocked at her actions, trying to find answers to why she did it. Pamela herself still had mental health issues and kept personalities concealed in her head, like skeletons in a closet. It certainly wouldn't take much to release her demons once more, only her love for Ruth kept them at bay.

A woman approached them dressed in a brown flowered top and plain dark green skirt; her long ginger hair was tied back with a yellow bobble. Her blue eyes concentrated on observing Ruth's face then she looked at the dressings on her arms.

"You must be Ruth" she said in a sickly sweet manner "I am Emma Williams"
"Yes and you are clearly from the psychiatric liaison team" Ruth said abruptly
"Do I detect a note of hostility in your voice" Emma replied sarcastically
"Fuck you" Ruth said scornfully
"You're a psychiatric nurse are you not?" Emma continued unfazed by Ruth's abusive remark

"Yes and I know the score, you ask me questions and being non judgmental psycho analyze me with your eyes and mind" Ruth said bitterly

"You have been modeling recently haven't you?" Emma said trying to gather more information.

"Yes and I'm a lesbian before you ask" Ruth felt herself getting angry

"Ruth listen to her she's trying to help you" Pamela interrupted

"Yes let me help you Ruth" Emma continued glancing at Pamela and back to Ruth.

"Ok but I understand where this is going and just want to go home" Ruth said addressing Emma and Pamela

"Yes we are but be patient and we can spend time abroad for a while" Pamela said smiling

"I will go now and visit you in a while Ruth ok?" Emma said moving away from the bedside

Pamela watched Emma disappear behind the curtains then looked at Ruth who held her head down in shame

"I suppose you think I'm stupid?" Ruth said in a low voice
"No you forget I've been there" Pamela said in an understanding tone.

"Yes but I have been looking after you and now I am the weak one" Ruth said ashamed

"Ruth we have come a long way and experienced so much together, I should have realized that all this glamorous life style is a bit much for you" Pamela said with empathy

"Yes but I didn't want to let you down, but I was worried about upsetting you and causing you to relapse" Ruth said gripping Pamela's hand

"I know and I think it's time to think of you and your needs and fuck mine" Pamela said with a smile
"It's all about us not me and that's what I want" Ruth said tearfully
"Yes let's deal with that ok?" Pamela agreed

Ruth was discharged from hospital on antidepressants and pain relief, she was confident that Pamela now understood her limitations as a model and they just worked on modeling for jewelry and clothes with a less demanding schedule away from the lime light. This suited Ruth and although Pamela found it mundane and boring she did it for Ruth's sake. Both of them were supporting each other working through nightmares and low moods together, they shared a common enemy in their past and dealt with it bravely together. The enemy was Pamela and Ruth's past traumas of abuse, this had haunted both women at various times and they both wore the scars beneath their skin.

Occasionally Ruth experienced Pamela's other identities, as she displayed them, but it was less frequent as she felt more secure with Ruth. The identity Anna the child appeared after Pamela had experienced a nightmare or some other sort of trauma. James was a rare identity these days as her angry episodes were few. Ruth experienced low moods and was on anti depressants and dealing with her condition. Pamela's memory was a problem as this was shared by her identities, Pamela, as the host would struggle to remember important events and often used a note pad in order to remember important things. When Ruth was with her she became her memory prompting her about times and dates.

As time went on the media that had criticized them for their open displays of lesbianism and public protests for gay liberation forgot them. The media found new victims to pester and intimidate, carefully avoiding racism, sexism and all kinds of prejudice remarks that caused such problems in the past. They were cunning but clever enough not to get sued by celebrities as they went on one witch-hunt after the other destroying people professional reputations and lives.

One of the worst parts of Pamela and Ruth's mental illness was the nightmares they occurred often and dominated both their lives. The images that the mind was capable of creating could be horrific and so real. Some were directly from experiences of their past, such as abuse from childhood or married life. There were the usual dreams of falling or flying which suggested trauma in their life or escaping from bad situations perhaps. Some interpretations indicated escapism. Often vampires or monsters were involved in their nightmares the figures that emerged from the darkness and terrorized them. These could easily have been their abusers from their childhood, ghosts from their past. Because it was so realistic one or the other would wake up screaming or find scratches on their body.

The dreams of medieval castles, maidens in distress or being carried off by dragons to caves were quite common. So were the vampire nightmares running in fear of their lives. Either Ruth would come to Pamela's rescue or vise versa. Even in the dreams they wore such elaborate costumes, such as a long dress with a high collar and a long sweeping cloak. Or small briefs over dark tights and shapely body Armour with shoulder pads.

One night Pamela dreamt of wearing a porcelain mask and being attacked by someone with a baseball, she is knocked to the ground and the mask is cracked while her head and face is covered with blood. After which a number of images of herself immerge out of her own body all wearing different clothes and some in uniform indicating her many identities. They appeared like ghostly spirits one wearing a black outfit with a veil, she lifts the veil to look at a grave stone of Ruth. Pamela wondered whether this was symbolic of Ruth's death, like a premonition. Sometimes Pamela would kneel beside the grave and place flowers by her grave. Another figure is in a wheelchair obviously Pamela's mother but Pamela is in the wheelchair being pushed about by Ruth.

All the images are her own identities none of them are the host. Even a child in a white night dress is Pamela as a child and often lost in some wood or in a dark room somewhere. A man is another image with her features he is looking down at his own penis or punching a wall. Sometimes a female soldier would appear brandishing a rifle or blade in a threatening manner.

Ruth's dreams were similar with similar outcomes death being one of them, usually her own. Ruth's dreams consisted of rats and spiders invading her personal space. Falling down a pit and dropping onto spiders, or snakes. Falling out of a tower or off a cliff. On a few occasions she was Pamela's mother crying for forgiveness sat in a wheelchair. Ruth's biggest fear was loneliness and so her worst nightmare was being alone somewhere like a station or bus stop.

Pamela and Ruth would wake up from a dream either screaming or crying. This resulted in comforting each other.

A vivid dream tended to make them think it was real and part of their lives after all the characters were there. The people in the dreams portrayed real characters from their past often features were exaggerated like that of cartoons; monsters were always huge and menacing. They always tried to escape but moved in slow motion as if they were stuck to the floor. Some dreams involved walking through many doors but never getting outside; as each door opened they entered another room.

Dreams could be interpreted in many different ways, but for those with a mental illness they become more complex and harder to understand. Most dreams can be related to the day's events known as recalling or recapping moments that mean something to you. A series of ideas can induce a combination of thoughts that formed some kind of story whether it is consistent or not.

People interpret dreams in various ways the idea of flying was generally to escape from a situation or place that you don't feel comfortable in. Often Pamela would witness Ruth being attacked and in her dreams raced to her rescue, but in some dreams she could actually see Ruth in an open casket surrounded with flowers like those they saw in the countryside on holiday. She would then see many familiar faces looking over the coffin some weeping. Then a parade of models walked around the grave just as if they were on the catwalk. This seemed to be all about Pamela's anxiety of losing Ruth and she often spoke to Ruth about this dream. Ruth had similar dreams about Pamela but often it involved a funeral at a crematorium with friends and family looking on.

In one nightmare Ruth had is was when she was walking on the catwalk when suddenly faced with masks each one falling from above, some smashing on to the ground. Images appeared before her wearing porcelain masks. Ruth pulls the masks off in frustration as she hates masks; behind each one is a person she knows. Behind the first mask was Pamela, the second Sheena, the third was Gloria and the fourth Emma her sister. But as she pulled off the final mask, Ruth saw Malcolm's face and then as she removed the mask he became angry and chased her down the catwalk. Ruth ran and ran until the stage ended, she then jumped off. Malcolm and her fell and landed on the ground amongst masks and the bodies of Malcolm's victims which lay all around them. Malcolm stood up and picked up his baseball bat, Ruth jumped to the left then to the right to avoid the bat. Malcolm hit the masks and bodies in a frenzied attack, his eyes were menacing as he began staring at Ruth. Then he hit another mask and this time the mask shattered and Pamela's face appeared, this changed into Pamela's mothers face Sarah, then disappeared. Ruth ran again but this time felt as if her feet were being weighed down by led, this time Malcolm caught up with her and hit her with his baseball bat, she noticed the blood splash and everything went black. She woke up and was quaking with fear. Pamela was looking at her and Ruth noticed that Pamela had blood on her face.

"Have I hurt you?" Ruth asked concerned
"No take a look at your legs" Pamela said alarmed

Ruth looked at her legs and then her hand which were also covered with blood
"My god I've been scratching myself" Ruth said horrified

"Yes let me help you clean yourself up" Pamela said "just like you did with me on the ward" Pamela actually remembered this."

Pamela got a damp flannel and cleansed Ruth's wounds, she reminded her of Ruth's activities in her sleep which explained how she received her injuries. She actually clung onto Pamela which accounted for the blood on Pamela and no wounds.

Pamela was known for the occasional sleep walking finding herself in odd places around the house, but sometimes returning safely to bed. She also had panic attacks and flash backs triggered by smells, seeing a person who reminds her of people from her past. Pamela was also a person who had compulsions and rituals; sometimes she would have mood swings for no apparent reason. The dreams seemed to enhance these conditions or behaviours escalating events out of all proportion, causing harm to her and sometimes others.

Pamela said although she had never taken drugs she had out of body experiences and sometimes hallucinations affecting one of the six senses usually visual. Ruth has been her rock stabilizing her along with her cocktail of medication and occasional therapy of some description. Ruth just needed to stay out of the limelight and hold on to what sanity she had left. Ruth tended to heal quickly and bounced back from her depressive state with support from Pamela. They were still in love and took their relationship to new heights.

THE POWER OF LOVE

*E*arly one morning on a baking hot morning in midsummer the phone rang in Pamela's apartment, it rang for a while before Pamela immerged from the bathroom covered in a bath robe and a towel wrapped around her head.

"Hello" Pamela said hesitantly "Oh hello Angela, how's Tara" she continued
"I'm fine, yes she's good too" Pamela said then nodded as she listened intently.

"I would love to but Ruth may not want to" she said looking at the bedroom door
Ruth had heard the phone and stood in her dressing gown with a worried look on her face.

"Let me get back to you ok?" Pamela said placing the phone on the receiver

Pamela began to miss being in the limelight, she loved performing in front of a crowd right from childhood when she was trained to walk the cat walk.

"Tara wants us to model cosmetics" Pamela said watching Ruth head towards the kitchen
"Really is that for magazines? Ruth asked
"Yes and for posters in shopping malls" Pamela continued "Not bad money"
"Ok" Ruth said eagerly "We need the money at the moment"
"Oh and she said there is a new fashion show being prepared" Pamela added
"You know how I feel about shows Pamela" Ruth slammed down her cup "I hate them"
"This is different" Pamela pleaded "It's a love thing and we could be great in this one"
"I am never going back on a cat walk" Ruth insisted
"Not even to tell the world that we are getting married" Pamela said confidently
"Married?" Ruth was puzzled "You want to marry me?"
"Yes a civil wedding maybe here and then honeymoon in Lake Garda in Italy" Pamela said positively

Ruth stood quietly for a while thinking about what she had said "Married"
"I am proposing to you Ruth" Pamela said smiling
"Well yes ok" Ruth replied smiling back
"The show is called 'The power of love' it's said to be big" Pamela continued excitedly
"Where is it?" Ruth asked
"It's a traveling show being staged in London, New York and Paris" Pamela added
"Makes me nervous just thinking about it" Ruth admitted
"Ruth you will be fine, it's going to be amazing, loads of celebrities and top models" Pamela tried hard to persuade Ruth.

"But I am not as confident as you and remember last time?" Ruth said trying to convince Pamela not to let her do it.

"But your stronger now and I will take better care of you this time" Pamela was very convincing.

"You said it's about love?" Ruth asked

"The power of love" Pamela said holding her arms up dramatically

"The power of love" Ruth asked "That's a song isn't it?"

"Yes I suppose so" Pamela said grinning

"So it's a show based on a song then?" Ruth asked

"Maybe, but what an idea and foundation for the fashion show" Pamela replied

"Sort of a hippy thing then based on sixties and seventies fashion no doubt" Ruth said with excitement

"Yes mixed with 21 century fashion" Pamela said equally excited by the thought of an infusion of 20th and 21st fashion ideas.

"Tara and Angela will be in the audience" Pamela announced with delight

Pamela managed to convince Ruth that it was advantageous to model in the show; it was more of a theatrical event judging by the costumes. Flower power using displays of flowers with hippie costumes performing to the Beatles song 'All you need is love' a fitting opening to the show.

The London show opened in the height of the summer with selection of models some that had performed many time and models that were new to the cat walk. Gloria Thompson, who was a friend of Pamela and Ruth, was at the show.

Gloria was a woman with mixed race parents, her father was a white Englishman and her mother was South African. Gloria had a coffee brown complexion and dazzling white teeth, with long black hair and stunning large brown eyes. Although she was heterosexual she believed in people living their lives as they want to and criticized no one. She lost a friend a few years ago called Kim who lost her battled against anorexia, collapsing on a catwalk during a show. Kim's parents were wealthy and sent her to a private school for her education. Kim could not fulfill her parent's expectations. So she became a model, but lost her life due to the complications of anorexia, her death was so tragic.

Pamela and Ruth faced their usual battle against some of the models who disagreed with their relationship. But they stuck together and had support of Gloria when it came to any disagreement. When they met Gloria she greeted them with open arms making more of a fuss of Ruth because she knew that she was struggling.

Gloria explained about Kim's last days with affection and knew that they would understand. Kim was feeling depressed as the press had hounded her about her condition. Facing Kim with her anorexia was like introducing a spider to someone who feared spiders. She suffered most of her life from this eating disorder, eventually her heart became weak and she died.

Family, friends and colleagues attended Kim's funeral; many models were there dressed in dark clothes looking far different from the outfits that they usually wore. Many of them were crying and some whispering to each other some discussing the funeral while others were more concerned with what people were wearing. The family remained together and refused to associate with the models, blaming them for leading Kim into modeling. The truth was that Kim herself wanted to be a model and chose her own career, she never wanted to follow her parent's lifestyle. Walking in her parents shadow was not option in her eyes, she had her own identity and it wasn't to be a spoilt little rich girl like some of her former friends.

Once the first show was filmed the press rushed to the stage doors to see Pamela and Ruth. One of them was the one who had caused them so many problems in the past. He was lingering around them like a vulture after his prey, hungry for a story he caught hold of Ruth's hand and spoke to her "So the lesbians are back" he said peering into her eyes

Ruth pulled away and surprisingly Gloria came to her rescue "Let her go you bastard" she shouted for all to hear

"So the blacks are lesbians this year" he said rudely
"How dare you insult her you fucking creep" Ruth shouted Pamela raced forward in her defense but Ruth had already slapped him and Gloria kicked him between the legs.

The reporter fell to the ground in pain and all three women cheered

Security guards escorted the reporter out of the building and he immediately hailed a taxi and disappeared down the street. The other reporters moved away from the women and pursued the other models. Hoping to gather stories from them instead, some of the models seemed pleased to provide them with what they needed. Discussing past experiences and enjoyment of appearing in the show.

The fashion critics were very keen to get good seats expecting to see more than fashion, as the title suggested. In fact 'the Power of love' fashion show was about more than fashion, it was a statement or underlying message about the freedom of choice. The object was to get rid of the stigmas surrounding the gay scene, mental health, racism and a whole array of prejudices that we face in the world today. It's all about loving yourself and others, expressing how you truly feel, and speaking out to the world.

Pamela was having her make up applied while Ruth was having her hair styled for her performance. The rooms were full of models being prepared for a magnificent show, their was hardly any conversation as most of the models appeared to be nervous, despite their many appearances on events like this. But this time it was different, because this show had raised more than the usual publicity, thanks to Pamela and Ruth, amongst others. This was the first time transsexual models appeared in a fashion show like this. Rocky horror had come to life making it more than a fashion show, selling more tickets than ever and providing the audience with incredible entertainment.

Some of the designs certainly agreed with the love scene displaying so many outfits from top designers. Some are bizarre and some earthier, with the use of many fabrics and other materials at their disposal. The outrageous were people wearing such things as toilet rolls stuck together on models head painted in silver, and a long dress made from cotton with a net curtain design over it. Alternatively one had a plain blue dress with large smarties all over it, traveling down in a coordinated fashion. The outrageous gave more freedom for ideas, as the models were more skimpily dressed with a more revealing demonstration of promiscuity. This left little to the imagination and the see through suit worn by Pamela was well viewed.

The evening wear was so romantic with evening dresses in all colours and designs, the dark blue off the shoulder look as demonstrated by Ruth, or the white and pink designs worn by Pamela contrasted with Sheena's green emerald dress with a matching emerald necklace and bracelet that seemed almost luminous. If this wasn't enough, there was the swimwear with exotic Hawaiian backdrop. The casual look was well received although it was less casual than last year and seemed to be a mixture of casual and formal so as to please the judges. There was then a cross match of cultures demonstrating the unity of nations, for example a mix of India and Europe, Japanese and German which was confusing at times. The wedding outfits showed that every sort of sexual persuasion was being addressed this demonstrated that the message that Pamela and Ruth were campaigning was finally being recognized and understood. The honeymoon was a little more farcical and almost gave the opposite message; Pamela and Ruth were not involved with this display and never modeled any of the outfits on this occasion.

The idea of mixing ancient history with the modern was not a new concept but effective when it came to fashion design much like tying rags in the hair and wearing sandal type shoes on their feet. The high wedge shoes wear popular and furs seemed a must for some designers. Long flowing skirts and hooded coats were also popular as well as the shades of pastel blending in many colours. Black and white stripes and squares in many patterns were shown in contrast with subtle shades of red or grey.

Ruth had become confident again and found that she was able to walk confidently on the catwalk in various costumes. Models respected her more as they did Pamela the whole idea of lesbians on a catwalk and certainly since the death of Kim, people's ideas of anorexia seemed to change. It was like the whole world had changed overnight although this was not the case, It was however the start of something new.

The backdrops were spectacular especially the love themes giant hearts everywhere, it was like 14th February Valentine's Day. Celebrities from around the globe attended. Pamela and Ruth were becoming very popularly all over the world. A rainbow tunnel was available that lit up as the models traveled under it, while various coloured confetti drifted down from above. The romantic evening showed a wonderful backdrop of a moonlit sky with many stars shining brightly against a black background.

Gloria wore outfits that complimented her beautiful coffee coloured skin tone at one point displaying a leopard style cat suit then contrasting this by wearing an evening gown in beige and cream with matching elegant jewelry. Sheena appeared with her wearing her favorite green velvet gowns. Each designer seemed happy with the way the models were displaying them on the catwalk, looks of contentment appeared on their faces. Smiles made it obvious that they were confident others would approve of their designs too.

Ruth's sister Emma was in the audience watching as Ruth appeared several times on the catwalk. Ruth was never aware that Emma was there until the last night when Emma waited for Ruth to appear back stage. Emma stood waiting watching each model pass her and head for the dressing room.

"Ruth" Emma shouted as she saw her approaching
Ruth hesitated and looked at Emma; Pamela nodded to her acknowledging her
"Hi Emma" She said politely.
"Hi Pamela" Emma replied smiling.
"Emma how are you?" Ruth said hesitantly
Ruth led Emma away to a quiet room
"Ruth I know its been two years but I have missed you"
"Me too" Ruth replied
"I do understand about you and Pamela and I am happy for you"
"What about mom and dad?" Ruth asked
"You know them I tried to explain things" Emma explained
"But don't hate them for it"
"I hate no one honestly" Ruth insisted
"Then come and see them please" Emma pleaded
"I will after the tour is over ok?" Ruth explained
Ruth embraced her sister they both shed a tear and both sat for a while talking about the show.
"You were brilliant in that show, you and Pamela" Emma said smiling
"It means a lot hearing that from you" Ruth said smiling back at her.
"I love London's fashion week its always appealed to me, the year they had the Egyptian theme" Emma said excitedly

"Elizabeth Taylor portrait of Cleopatra as an idea for fashion and introducing a modern slant on it" She added.
"Yes that year was good" Ruth agreed
"Pamela looked good in her silver and black outfit" Emma continued, "You make a great couple and perform well on the catwalk together.

After a short while Pamela entered the room and seemed to address them both "Are you hungry?" She asked, "Shall we go for lunch somewhere?"
Ruth looked at Pamela and then at Emma "Shall we?".
Emma nodded "Yes that would be nice" she agreed.
They all left the room and headed to the exit, across the street stood a series of restaurants. They headed across the road "Indian or Chinese?" Ruth asked
"Chinese if that's ok" Emma said waiting for the others to agree.
They chose a nice quiet cubical area and sat comfortably surrounded by a few people on other tables. An American couple sat in the next cubical and were talking loudly as if they wanted them to here their conversation.

"The fashion show was fine but the god damn Lesbians spoilt it as usual" The woman said spitting venom
"Well if our daughter was like that I would disown her," The man said dismissively.
Ruth looked at Pamela with an angry expression, but to their amazement Emma responded
"What a pair of ignorant tossers, don't they understand anything". Emma shouted.
"Leave it Emma, its not worth it" Ruth said trying to prevent trouble

"We get this crap all the time, we are used to it" Pamela said looking at the menu.

The Americans left the restaurant soon afterwards and the women placed their order.
Emma was still annoyed by their comments and continued to discuss it with Pamela and Ruth.

"I really didn't know what you were going through" Emma said "I feel so bad because I too was negative about you" Emma bowed her head in shame.

"Come on Emma you were driven by other peoples opinion, influenced by their thoughts". Ruth said in an understanding manner.
"Some people can be very persuasive, using pier pressure and all that sort of thing".
"I realize that now but what about mom and dad?" Emma asked.
"They may never understand because of their generation" Ruth replied.
"Anything out of the norm is considered odd, my mother would never understand either" Pamela said sadly
"Is she dead?" Emma asked.
Pamela looked at Ruth "Yes in a way she is". Pamela said, "She was murdered"
"My god no way" Emma said in an empathetic manner
"Yes and the killer is still at large" Pamela added
"The one that has been killing so many people?" Emma asked.
"Who knows" Ruth answered swiftly

The food soon arrived and nothing more was said about the murder of Pamela's mother. Instead the conversation changed to more discussion about the fashion show and about holidays. The evening seemed to go quickly Pamela and Ruth took Emma back to her hotel and they both hugged Emma.

"Don't forget my invitation to your wedding" Emma said
"Of course Emma" Ruth replied, "You will all get one".
"Take care Emma" Pamela said "see you soon".
Emma looked at Pamela strangely when she this as if she would never see her again. Emma thought she could see a strange light around her head almost like a halo. It was odd because Emma had often had dreams of Angels ever since Pamela visited her parents home all that time ago. It freaked her out then as it did now, something was clearly wrong in her eyes but she was unable to convey it or express why she felt weird.

The show was a great success in London and Paris; audiences were entertained by the 'love theme' although they had mixed feelings about the types of sexual persuasions displayed in the show. The stigma remained with some people who criticized the gay acts who dressed so elegantly on the catwalk. On the last night in of the show in New York Pamela announced the engagement of Ruth and herself to a television reporter. She announced a civil wedding in England on their return, which was frowned upon by the public and media alike. It seemed although they were accepted for who they were marriage was too extreme.

The news reached England and soon became news headlines, many people saw the news and television programs wanted to book them on their show. Once again they were being interviewed and found they were popular again. Pamela was watching the interviewers body language while Ruth was talking

"You speak to us about normality and I say what's normal about the so called Christian society pushing out lesbian, gays and transsexuals like they don't count"

"Yes and what about the media who hound people for stories about anorexia or other illnesses forcing them to take their lives"

The bishop leaned forward already red in the face "Christianity is as it always will be opposed to homosexuality and the media help to display this". He pointed his finger at Pamela and Ruth "Your display of lesbianism only demonstrates the meaning of the bible regarding abstaining from fornication and so banish such wicked behaviour from society"
"Fucking hypercritic bastard" Ruth said angrily "Your sort mess with little boys and call us wicked how dare you"
"Look at the profanities displayed by these women doesn't that say it all" The bishop said addressing the audience
Ruth rose from her seat and walked towards him, security moved in quickly
Pamela walked forward pulling Ruth back "Don't let these ignorant fuckers upset you they are not worth it" Pamela said moving her back to her seat.
"Let them have their say" The vicar insisted
"I speak for all people who are suppressed by the bullies of society".

"So who are the bullies and who are the suppressed?" the interviewer asked

"The suppressed are anyone who could be deemed as different" Pamela said "But god bod just want these people away out of sight"

"Yes and the bullies are people like that wanker over there who thinks he himself is god, a true narcissi full of his own importance". Ruth said trying to remain in her seat despite her mood.

"Clearly you are an example of lower class scum and have no connection with the real world" The bishop said dismissing them with the wave of his hand

"Oh well Mr Bishop let me tell you that you are the one that is delusional and out of touch with reality" Ruth stood up again and Pamela stood beside her

"What an arrogant jumped up prick you are, get your head out of your arse and join the real world where people like us do exist". Pamela said pointing at him

"Centuries ago you people would be burnt at the stake as witches". The bishop said angrily

"Oh that's a bit extreme" the vicar said laughing

"There you have it old fashioned methods from old fashioned views" Ruth shouted

"I am sure the audience think society needs a broom up its arse Pamela shouted

The audience applauded upsetting the bishop

"See how the devils children influence his flock, society needs to be rid of such people before society is destroyed". The bishop continued

"I say get rid of religion and politics and your half way there to having a descent society" Ruth shouted in anger.

"Yes get rid of those who dictate about what we should eat, wear and act in society according to religion". Pamela added
Again the audience applauded and watched as Pamela and Ruth left the stage they then returned with people with anorexia, transsexuals and people with various deformities.

Pamela then took centre stage and looking at the religious elements across the stage announced, "These people want to be part of your society with your help they can be". Pamela's words seemed to echo out into the audience as they all stood up and clapped
"There's your answer bishop Ruth said watching him and the other religious leaders leave the stage.

On another show Pamela and Ruth was invited to a morning show, which was broadcast nationwide and watched, by millions of people. The presenter introduced the program and spoke positively about the power of love fashion show.

"The power of love show proved to be successful in London" The presenter said "How do you think it will go in Paris and the United States?"
"I imagine it will be as successful as it was in London" Pamela said confidently
"The power of love is about unity and love in many ways be it heterosexual, homosexual transsexual or any other way, across the world" Ruth said
"So why shouldn't it be a success, fashion is not just about style and elegance its about making a statement" Pamela stated pointing to a poster of Ruth and herself in stylish evening gowns.

A few designers were introduced to discuss the power of love show from the prospective of the designers and their styles and up and coming costumes including imaginative ideas. One of the designers introduced Sheena as she modelled a few outfits on the stage. Other models helped to display other designer's outfits and the show ended with Pamela and Ruth announcing their engagement. The presenter congratulated them and spoke about the show going to Russia, she mentioned a diplomatic reason to visit Moscow and discuss the power of love in order to unite the world.

Ruth realised that Malcolm was a violent psychopath; he had all the signs such as no shame in what he did. Ruth was the only one in his life and she could have no family or friends round her. He displayed acts of selfishness, he was lazy, harmful and immoral acting as if this was normal and acceptable. Ruth began to wonder why she hadn't seen this before in him and recognised the signs of a psychopath. Perhaps she could have acted more swiftly and prevented things happening as they did. It then occurred to her that he was capable of raping and killing Pamela's mother.

Malcolm intentionally and methodically murdered women and was still free to continue to do so. He roamed the streets at night searching for Ruth hiding in shadows and hoping that one night Ruth would appear.

Malcolm came out of the suburbs into and began to search for the women once more. He was annoyed by the news that Pamela and Ruth were to be married and wanted to discuss this with Ruth. Malcolm had become a serial killer and a psychopath. He went to Ruth's apartment first hoping to find her there, lingering around the corner waiting to follow her into her apartment.

Pamela continued to have nightmares of Ruth being murdered by Malcolm with his baseball bat, killed just like those innocent women who resembled them. The police never found the killer and

So the murders remained unsolved.

Malcolm finally caught up with Pamela and Ruth as they entered Pamela's apartment. He had only seen Ruth enter the door and followed her up to the apartment. He was close enough to stop the door from shutting with his foot and then pushed his way inside. Ruth tried to prevent him from entering but he was too strong and forced her away from the door.

Ruth ran across the room and Malcolm caught up with her, punching her in the face, she fell back onto the settee and he raised his baseball bat to hit her. At that moment she screamed blood trickling from her nose. Suddenly he let out a yell as Pamela plunged a knife into his back she was shouting in a deep voice at him, but nothing made sense. Malcolm staggered to the floor trying to get the knife out of his back. The knife eventually dropped onto the floor and landed beside Malcolm who lay bleeding and groaning.

Pamela helped Ruth to her feet and dialed emergency services, as she did so she smelt Malcolm's after shave and froze on the spot realizing he was her mother's murderer. Memories of her mother's rape and murder came flooding back. Ruth stroked her hair "its ok your safe" she said confidently

At that moment Malcolm rose to his feet and ran at Ruth with the knife firmly in his hand Pamela pushed Ruth out of the way and Malcolm plunged the knife into Pamela's stomach.

Pamela fell back and Ruth shouted "No!"
Ruth grabbed the baseball bat and hit him repeatedly over the head, then Pamela and her leaped forward and pushed Malcolm over the balcony and he fell to his death.

Pamela fell to the ground holding her stomach the blood seeped through her clothes. Ruth grabbed a table cloth and tried to stop the bleeding. The colour drained from Pamela's face as she lay in Ruth's arms tears rolling down her cheeks.

"Don't go, I can't live without you" Ruth said crying
But Pamela was weak and eventually let go of her hand

"Stay with me Pamela, I need you" Ruth pleaded

But Pamela closed her eyes and died

The police entered the apartment followed by Kathy, who had been contacted by Ruth earlier. Ruth was rocking with holding Pamela firmly in her arms and she was mumbling nursery rhymes.

Kathy knelt beside Ruth with her hand on her shoulder and began talking to her

"Ruth its Kathy" she said trying to get her attention
"I am not Ruth, I am Sarah" She announced
"Come on Ruth lets sort you out" Kathy said trying to free her from Pamela
"Stop calling me Ruth" she shouted, "I am Sarah"

One of the policemen tried to help Kathy to free Ruth from Pamela as the ambulance crew arrived, but Ruth held her firmly and continued rocking back and forth.

"Don't touch her, go away" she shouted

Kathy looked up at the ambulance crew and then the police "Give us a few minutes please" Kathy said tearfully.

Kathy held onto Ruth as the ambulance crew took Pamela away, Ruth remained silent staring into space with a fixed expression on her face. After Pamela had left Kathy got Ruth ready to leave the apartment, they walked down the stairs and Kathy noticed the tape around the area where Malcolm had fallen. Close to this was a black body bag, which contained Malcolm's dead body.

Ruth didn't seem to be aware of anything not even Kathy who was escorting her into a van. Ruth did turn her head and appear to look up at the apartment but then looked back and returned to her blank expression. Things had happened so fast from their final show to the last moments that Pamela and Ruth shared together. From Pamela's admission to the beginning of their relationship Kathy was trying to rationalize the entire event in order to relay it to the police. She was the one that had to explain everything to them and to Ruth's family. As for Pamela's relatives they needed to know a lot about what went on as Pamela never kept in touch with them.

Kathy went with Ruth to a psychiatric ward close to the one where her and Kathy worked. She was greeted by a nurse there and led to a quiet lounge area near the office. Kathy sat Ruth down and watched as Ruth drew her knees up and grabbed them with her hands and began rocking just as Pamela once did. Ruth then sang nursery rhymes over and over again.

Kathy began speaking to the nurse "Hi Gill, you know Ruth don't you?"
Gill nodded "Yes Kathy, Its very sad to see her like this"
"My best friend reduced to this" Kathy replied
"I can't believe it poor lady" Gill said looking at her rocking.
"Take care of her for me" Kathy said looking at Gill then Ruth
"I will and come here whenever you like Kathy" Gill offered
"Thank you" Kathy said squeezing Gills hand as she walked away

Kathy looked back at Ruth in the lounge and then left the door, she walked down the corridor to the main entrance and passed the security officer. As she left the building she looked back at the ward where Ruth was staying her thoughts drifted back to Pamela's admission and the start of Pamela and Ruth's relationship. She couldn't help thinking that maybe Ruth would have been well if it hadn't been for Pamela. But then if it hadn't been Pamela maybe it would have been someone else, perhaps Ruth was just one of those nurses who cared too much. As for the love affair, did that truly exist or was it all one sided. Pamela saw her mother in Ruth and maybe that was all, Ruth on the other hand loved

Pamela but this could have been transference and again not true love.

No one but Pamela and Ruth could ever answer to whether or not they were truly in love. They were fighting to be accepted in society as lesbians and began to be finally recognized when Pamela was murdered. Kathy wept as she walked through the car park she took a final look back at the ward and entered her car. After a short spell sitting in the car she drove away out of the hospital and towards her home.

The next day Kathy returned on her day off, she brought with her Ruth's mother Diane and two sisters Emma and Claire. Claire was Ruth's younger sister who was at college, she slim with dark hair and was very smartly dressed. They entered the ward after going through the security checks, Ruth's mother seemed particularly nervous constantly looking around her just like Ruth did when she first entered a ward.

Kathy pointed at a room where Ruth was sat staring into space, she was rocking just as she did when she was at Pamela's apartment. Emma was the first to approach the room she kissed Ruth on the forehead and hugged her, but Ruth did not respond. Then Diane kissed and hugged her and still there was no response. Finally Claire moved forward and kissed her, Ruth stopped rocking and tears began to trickle from her eyes.

"What's wrong with her?" Claire asked
"She's suffering from depression" Kathy replied
"Can I speak to you?" Diane asked

Kathy led Diane out of the room leaving Emma and Claire who were sitting either side of Ruth. Diane looked at Kathy then into the room where her daughters were sat.

"Have I been so bad that I have to be punished like this?" Diane asked
"Why do you say this?" Kathy replied
"What a bloody mess" Diane said touching her forehead with her right hand.
"What do you mean?" Kathy asked
"You know about the abuse?" Diane said in a low voice
"Yes Ruth told me some time ago" Kathy said puzzled
"Well I was told first by Ruth, I thought she was attention seeking and ignored it" Diane stared at Kathy "Me, her own mother, turned her away" she looked back at Ruth "I caused all this because I turned her away again when she needed my support"
"But" Kathy was interrupted by Diane as she continued to explain
"That's not all" Diane said "She kept a diary every year and wrote about events, its all in there, what he did and the fact that I wouldn't listen."
"She doesn't blame you Diane, I know that."
"So what will happen to her?
"She will get help, but its up to you to support her now ok" Kathy advised her.
"Yes I will, I promise", Diane seemed very positive "Just make her well again".

The ward was particularly busy a by polar (manic depressive) patient was running up and down the ward, a girl was screaming and patients were walking into a smoke filled room. A man was sat staring into space speaking to himself, while a lady walked slowly down the corridor escorted by a member of staff. Diane went back to sit with Ruth Emma moved so that she could sit beside her, Diane held Ruth's hand and was speaking to her.

Kathy knew that there was nothing else that she could do, so she went to the office and spoke to the staff. There was no mention of Ruth's father and it became increasingly obvious that he was no longer with the family. Kathy presumed that there was far more to the abuse story than even she knew, perhaps the diary revealed more than anyone knew. Diane was well aware of the truth, but even now chooses to tell no one. Ruth was the one person who could reveal the facts, but was not in a position to say anything.

Emma left the room searching for the toilet, when she entered the cubical the lavatory bowl was covered with blood. There were blood stained footprints on the floor and as she looked in the mirror she froze on the spot. There in front of her was a reflection of Pamela dressed in white with a shining halo over her head, just like she had seen many times before. Pamela was clutching her stomach and not speaking, blood was oozing from through her fingers. Emma let out a scream and staff rushed into the room, there was no blood around and no evidence of any activity in the area.

Ruth turned to her mother and gazed into her eyes "Mother!" she said clearly, Diane embraced her and wept. Kathy looked on, holding onto Emma who was also weeping. Ruth's brother David had joined them and was sitting next to Claire, they seemed bewildered by all the activity. Emma was trying to make sense of what she saw, it was so real yet there was no evidence of anyone being there in the toilet with her.

Ruth and Pamela

Influential songs that inspired me to write this book

Beautiful	Christina Aguilera
Billy Jean	Michael Jackson
Theme S express	s express
Girl on fire	Alicia Keys
All about us	Tatu
Fashion	David Bowie
Your song	Ellie Golding
All you need is love	Beatles
Falling	Julee Cruise Dream sequence 'Twin peaks'
Power of love	Gabrielle Aplin
42	Cold play
Girls just wanna have fun	Cyndi Lauper
Children	Robert Miles
Breakaway	Kelly Clarkson
Time warp	Rocky horror show
Not gonna get us	Tatu

(Don't fear) the reaper	Blue oyster cult
Who wants to live forever	Queen
That's what you get	Paramore
Resurrection	PPK
Phoenix burning	Tangerine dream

MESSAGE TO READERS

The reason for writing this book was to bring people into awareness of mental health and the need to communicate with people with mental health condition. It shows that everybody has a right to live in society and should not be ignored.

I would also like to point out that although I am heterosexual I do recognize the fact that some people are Lesbian, Bisexual, Gay and transsexual. Whatever peoples sexual leaning they have the right to be recognized in society and should feel free to be part of the world.

It is everybody's given right to live freely without society, to speak and act freely without fear of condemnation. I exercise my freedom of speech by writing this book some may find this offensive, but in order to introduce realism into the story, it has been necessary to use swear words and elements of violence.

A study of various relationships enabled me to understand more about them and helped to form the story of Pamela and Ruth's lesbian relationship. I must also add that some aspects of this book are taken from personal experience, which I found difficult to write.

I hope that by writing this book I have succeeded in providing people with a clearer understanding of the type of life that exists on a mental health ward, in the community and behind the scenes in the modeling world.

Printed in Great Britain
by Amazon.co.uk, Ltd.,
Marston Gate.